ASHER

INTERGALACTIC DATING AGENCY

DRAGON BRIDES
BOOK SEVEN

KATE RUDOLPH

Copyright © 2023 by Kate Rudolph

All rights reserved.

No part of this book may be reproduced in any form or by any electronic or mechanical means, including information storage and retrieval systems, without written permission from the author, except for the use of brief quotations in a book review.

ABOUT ASHER

Asher knows what he wants and a mate isn't part of the bargain. But when his boss turns her marriage minded meddling his way, he's forced to take a meeting with the Intergalactic Dating Agency. There's no way the matchmaker can find a lady who will meet his exacting standards. Then Zoe Gershwin crashes into his life and chaos ensues.

Zoe's playing the hottest new Alternate Reality game and it's so realistic she'd almost believe she's really in space. There's a hot dragon lord, an alien planet, and really strange game mechanics. It has to be a game, otherwise it means Zoe's been abducted by aliens and plopped down on a strange planet a long way from home. How is she supposed to get out of this mess?

When the dragon lord makes an offer, it's her only way home. But why does he need a fake fiance? And can she play the part and keep her hands to herself?

CHAPTER ONE

Everything on Vemion was soft, and it made Asher want to scowl. They didn't have time to waste on VMC12, and he dreaded to think how the three days spent away from work would put him behind schedule. Was Remy taking care of the air filtration issue? What about the infestation of those damned lizkats?

His fingers clenched the teacup in his hand hard enough that he feared he'd break the delicate porcelain. He set the cup down silently and checked his watch. This meeting was already five minutes late.

Did the matchmaker treat everyone like this? Was it some kind of test? He'd flown halfway across the system because she'd found viable brides for six of his cousins. Unfortunately, she refused to take initial meetings over video link, so he'd been forced to come to Vemion.

He yanked his comm out of his pocket and made a note to ask Remy about repairs to the water treatment building. Yes, he'd left a list for her, and his sister was more than capable of following instructions, but Asher hadn't slept the night before, his mind reeling with everything that could go wrong while he was away.

Truthfully, he hadn't had an uninterrupted night of sleep since his first week on VMC12, when Lady Nova left him in charge of the place while she went to act as governor for another colony.

It would be years, maybe a decade or more, until VMC12 had enough terraformed land to need a governor or any ruling council. And if Asher played it right, that would be him.

Lord-Governor Asher had a nice ring to it.

A title he'd earned, rather than the one that had been handed to him at birth. Land of his own to rule. People to govern.

He clutched the comm tight and made another note and cursed himself for this waste of time. Lady Nova had *ideas* about marriage and family. She insisted that a young man should seek a bride to prove he was settled and capable of taking on more responsibility. With all three of her sons paired off, her eyes had turned to another project, and it was Asher who was right there.

He didn't have time to woo a woman. The women on VMC12 were just a busy as he was, and few of them were of the same rank. Wasting his time speaking with the matchmaker would save him time later, and it was the only reason he hadn't walked out yet.

The silk curtain at the back of the room fluttered and then was swept aside by a middle-aged woman with brown skin, dark hair, and striking blue eyes. She wore a diaphanous lavender robe cinched at the waist with a wide green belt inlaid with gold thread. She wouldn't have been out of place in the king's court.

"Lord Asher, forgive me for the delay." She glided across the room and took a seat on the couch on the opposite side of the low table from him. "I had to deal with a pressing matter. Thank you for your patience and agreeing to meet in my office. I am Shade."

Asher kept his face calm. He even managed a neutral smile. This woman had something he wanted and he couldn't castigate her for making him wait an extra ten minutes on top of the day long flight to get here. "Of course, I'm glad you had an opening for me."

Shade's eyes flicked up and down, taking him in, then they went distant for a moment, and she shook her head just enough to jostle the decorative pins in her hair. "Interesting," she murmured, so low that he didn't think he was meant to hear it. Then she poured her own cup of tea and sipped. "Your inquiry said you're looking for a wife."

"Yes, I am." Why else would he visit a matchmaker? "I require a poised lady who is willing to take up residence on VMC12 once it's open to settlers. It would be acceptable if she prefers to maintain separate households until then, but I require marriage within the year and will need her to visit from time to time. She needs to be someone who can entertain herself. I'm a busy man and I'm building a planet, I don't have time for a wi—" He snapped his mouth shut and took a deep breath before speaking again. "I don't have time for distractions."

Shade didn't seem to mind that his requirements lacked romance. She took another sip of tea before putting her cup down. "It sounds to me like you don't much want a wife at all."

True. All too true. But he wasn't about to admit that. "I'm thirty-two years old and establishing myself. It's time." He tried to ignore that Lady Nova had expressed that exact sentiment to him once. But she was right.

"Do you wish for a sexual relationship with this

wife of yours?" Shade asked, "or is this merely a convenient arrangement?"

"Excuse me?" It wasn't any business of hers what kind of arrangement he had.

Shade sighed. "Lord Asher, you don't want a wife, you want a convenient woman to trot out at dinner parties. There are plenty of women who would be content with such an arrangement, but not all of them are looking for carnal marriages. If you want me to find the perfect woman for you—"

"An adequate one will do," he interrupted, unable to stop himself.

"I take pride in my work, your lordship, adequate will not do for *me*." Shade leaned back and took him in again. "I have some skill in locating mates, I could look for yours."

"Absolutely not." Asher refused to go down that road. Fated mates felt like something out of a children's story, even if he'd met plenty of mated couples. He didn't need some divine force of the universe pointing out the perfect person for him. He feared he'd only be a disappointment to such a woman. He couldn't run his colony and be the dragon his mate needed, not unless the universe had designated a *convenient woman to trot out at dinner parties*, as Shade had put it.

If it upset Shade to hear it, she didn't say. "Very well. Our subsequent meetings can be done over comms. I will do some research and contact you about our next steps. If all goes well, by next week you'll meet the first candidate. Is that satisfactory?"

"I'll need her to come to VMC12, I can't waste time travelling back and forth from Vemion." Any woman unwilling to endure that small inconvenience would never make it as his wife.

Shade nodded. "That's acceptable." Then she paused. "And about the nature of your relationship? I will need to know."

Asher couldn't remember the last time he'd gone to bed with a woman. He'd been so busy for the past two years that most nights he collapsed exhausted into bed to suffer fitful sleep. It would be unfair to inflict that on a wife. "I have no need for love and I would never force someone to endure my attentions."

"Very well, your lordship. I shall find you an *adequate* wife. Have a nice day."

Outside, the air was clear and the sun shone brightly. Asher had to pause in a small park, tipping his head back and breathing deep. The air on VMC12 had to be treated to remove particulate matter kicked up by the terraformers and it never smelled fresh. He only remembered what he was missing out on when he visited home.

All the more reason to stay away.

He'd arrived late last night and dumped his things at his brother Knox's townhouse in the city. Asher was in no hurry to get back, even though delay might make him miss the transport back to the colony. And if he missed that, he'd be stuck here for another week until the next supply ship went out.

There'd be no avoiding the horde then.

Asher loved his family. He worked with his sister Remy every day. He kept in contact with his fellow triplets, Flint and Knox, most weeks. But that wasn't all. He had three other siblings and two well-meaning but interfering parents. Living on the other side of the system was an act of self-preservation as much as ambition. Luckily, everyone except Flint and Knox was spending time at the summer palace and would have no idea he'd been on Vemion until he was back on the colony.

Knox's townhouse was in the ugly New Modern style that was sweeping through the city. It was all about the marriage of harsh lines and lush curves and always looked to Asher like something had gone very wrong in the planning. All the windows looked a bit like mushrooms, with perfectly square bottom frames that were hooded with arched glass on the top. And the style wasn't restricted to the architecture, no, it was painted in the same clash of color and shape.

It made the utilitarian compound on VMC12 seem calm and inviting rather than sterile.

The front door flung open and Knox and Flint scrambled out, each of his brothers engulfing him in a hug strong enough to knock the air out of his chest. "Sneaking here in the middle of the night!" Knox slapped him on the back. "Who raised you?"

Asher glared at his brother and flicked invisible dirt off of his collar. His brothers were dressed as if they'd just come from the sparring ring, and Flint had a smudge of dirt on his cheek. If it weren't for the clothes and for Knox's extra muscles, they were identical. It had driven their tutors to madness and led to more than one prank in their Academy days.

Asher had missed his brothers. "I couldn't change the transport schedule," he said, though it wasn't exactly true. Asher *could* have booked a private flight, but he didn't see the point in the extra expense when every credit counted.

Flint flung an arm around his shoulders and practically dragged him inside. "Of course, of course. You're far too responsible for your own good. Now, come on, we're drinking the expensive stuff. You know Knox is good for it."

"Not the Elysian Whiskey!" Knox yelled from behind them. "There are only four bottles of that in the galaxy and I'm savoring it."

Knox was a collector of... everything, as far as Asher could tell. As long as it was costly and rare, he wanted it. It gave his townhome a museum-like feel to see everything on display, but Asher was glad his brother had a hobby. And, unlike Flint's penchant for fast flying and sleek space ships, Knox's was, at least, safe.

The dining room was piled high with enough food for a village, most of Asher's favorites. The farms on VMC12 weren't yet producing anything but the hardiest vegetables, and while they imported a lot of food from Vemion, it tasted better fresh.

"Tell us about your bride," Flint demanded between bites of some sort of meat slathered in sauce. "You know that just about every lady we know would break under Lady Nova's gaze." He shuddered at the mention of Asher's boss.

Asher threw a breadstick at him. "The matchmaker is doing research, I'm not engaged yet."

"But why would you *want* to be?" Knox asked. His

feet were propped on the table with his hands behind his head. "You'll make her miserable."

Flint chucked the breadstick at Knox. "Don't be mean to Ash."

"Lady Nova is hardly at the colony to approve, and I don't want to move my wife—" He had to pause for a second after saying that, it was too strange to contemplate. But he continued, "—to suffer in a place not ready for society. Once I'm Lord-Governor, she can join me there on a permanent basis."

His brothers made sarcastic, awed noises at his ambitions. Asher rolled his eyes.

"Name one thing you even like about that place," Knox demanded.

"Remy's there." Easy enough. Remy was his youngest sister and his second youngest sibling. She'd been the one he was closest to outside of Flint and Knox and there was no one he could count on more than her.

"Remy could be anywhere," said Flint. "What about something that's not a person you literally share blood with?"

If he said anything, it would lead to an argument. It always did. Flint and Knox, their parents, and the rest of their siblings—except for Remy—were convinced that he was wasting his life on a barren rock past the edge of civilization. He wasn't making discoveries, he wasn't hoarding jewels, he wasn't doing anything that a properly programmed robot couldn't do.

And he wasn't going to think about how the same could be said about his requirements for a wife.

"Can we enjoy dinner before I head to port?" he asked. This time when he reached for a breadstick, he ate it.

"Port?" Knox practically fell out of his seat. "You just got here! Tell me you'll stay the night."

"Sorry, I can't. I was only able to stay the full day because the ship had routine safety maintenance. It leaves this evening. I need to return to VMC12 before Remy sends out bounty hunters to drag me back." Neither of his brothers smiled at that.

"You never call it home," Flint murmured.

"What?" His brother was talking nonsense.

But Knox agreed with him. "You've lived in that place for more than two years now, and I've never heard you call it home. You don't want to be there."

"It's where I'm needed." And it was where years of hard work would finally pay off. One day he'd be governor and prove to everyone that he was more than a spoiled younger son.

Flint opened his mouth, but closed it when Knox

shook his head. That silent communication was something the three of them had done to others their entire lives, and now these two were doing it to him. Asher tried not to feel left out.

But after that, dinner conversation was stilted, and when he left for the port, neither of his brothers offered to give him a ride. Which was fine. Asher didn't need to bother them.

And as soon as he got *home* on VMC12, everything would be back to normal.

For some reason that didn't make him feel any better.

CHAPTER TWO

A GIANT HISSING bug launched itself at Zoe and would have knocked her back if she hadn't dodged out of the way in time. Her ears rang with the echo of the screech and she gave her head a bit of a shake. No time to waste now, not if she was going to make this mission a success.

She was moving too fast. Her instincts screamed at her to run, to clear every room before the creepy-ass alien bugs had a chance to converge on her and do whatever it was that creepy-ass alien bugs did to innocent humans who didn't like creepy crawlies.

It couldn't be clearer where her destination lay. She heard the whispering echoes of whimpers and the only remaining light overhead flickered and seemed to point her deeper down the hallway to a large door covered in childish stickers and drawings.

The nursery.

This ship carried families between space stations, or it had, before the creepy bugs, and those families had children.

Now she was hearing the cries of a lot of orphans. She couldn't save their families, but she could and *would* save the kids.

She whipped around and looked for more of the creepy-crawlies, but the hallway was empty for now. Good. Since she'd passed the last checkpoint she'd have a bit of a breather to figure out the lock. Because, of course, the door was locked.

Zoe studied the stickers on the outside, looking for a clue that might tell her which of the buttons to push to get the door to slide open. Her heartbeat was in overdrive, convinced that she'd be bug food if she didn't speed up. But she couldn't freak out yet. If she didn't figure it out... well.

No time to waste.

Her right ear tingled, and it drew her gaze to scratches around the door handle. A circle. Okay. A clue? The circle seemed to lead in a straight line to a square, then another circle, then a triangle.

Circle. Square. Circle. Triangle.

Zoe pressed the corresponding shapes, but the indicator light above the lock didn't change. What had she missed? She looked at the pattern again and cursed as she realized her mistake.

Circle. *Line*. Square. Circle. Triangle.

The light changed to green and the door slid open to reveal a room full of orphans and a towering space-warrior who had his blaster out and was facing the door, ready to defend the kids until his dying breath.

"Zoe, you've saved us," he said in that echoing rumble that she'd been chasing through the past three missions. "Let me—"

The screen in front of her eyes went black and the timer beeped. With a frustrated groan, Zoe ripped off the headset her phone was attached to and stared at her computer.

The data was done compiling.

No more fun and games.

Zoe shot a guilty glance towards her office door. It was as firmly shut as ever. She was stuck in the basement of the astronomy building with no window, and in an office she was pretty sure had been a utility closet until some enterprising PhD student of years past had claimed it as their own. She could get her work done down here without interruption.

And no one knew when she took a bit of a break to play *Space Warrior Sigma*.

The *Sigma* breaks were becoming more and more common, and Zoe was doing her best not to think about *why*. Three years into her PhD, and it felt like she wasn't making any progress.

"I'll still be a doctor someday, Mom," she muttered to the picture of her smiling mother. Her mom had been so excited when Zoe was accepted into this program and when the same cancer she'd fought when Zoe was a kid came back, her mom had forbidden her from delaying her program to go back home and help.

Maybe her mom had known there was no fighting the disease this time. Or maybe she'd known that Zoe wouldn't have gone back to school when she was shrouded in grief for the woman who'd raised her.

Zoe would trade the last three years and much more for one more day with her mom.

"Damn it." She swiped at the stupid tear that had dared to fall and grabbed one of the sticky note pads on her desk. She tore one off and stuck the bright orange paper over her mom's picture.

A clump of Zoe's straight black hair had fallen out of her scrunchie and she redid it all with the practice of a woman who'd had long hair all her life.

Maybe it was time for a new haircut. Maybe that kind of change would be enough to stave off the yawning chasm of emptiness inside of her that she wasn't willing to face.

Zoe stared at the numbers on the screen for several moments and had to blink a few times, hoping that would help them make sense. She'd wanted to be an astronomer since she was eight years old, something she'd known since her mom took her to watch the sky through the local university's gigantic telescope.

Well, actually Zoe had wanted to be the person to discover alien life and then go live on another planet with an alien prince.

Mapping stars was as close as things got to that in the real world. The rest of it she had to live vicariously through games.

And Zoe loved games. Whether it was playing them on her console back home, loading them up in her 3D headset and playing them on her phone, or discovering pop-up live games that immersed her in the experience in ways a console never could, she was always searching out the newest thing.

Speaking of...

Zoe checked the clock and grinned. Her data could

wait until tomorrow. She had a date with an escape room.

At least that's what she thought it was. She'd seen the ad popup on social media a few weeks ago promising an *out of this world experience* with *never before seen technology* and a prize she couldn't imagine. It was all marketing, obviously. She was trying her best not to get her hopes up. Especially since it might turn out to be some sort of dating sim.

What kind of space game was *Intergalactic Dating Agency: Off World Adventure?*

She was going to find out soon. Zoe shut her computer down and locked the office behind her, as if one of the other grad students cared enough about her work to try and steal it. They'd be more likely to steal the sticky notes, and Zoe would defend those with her life, or a dinky lock that stuck when it got too humid.

The university was in the center of the city and Zoe was grateful, as it meant she didn't need a car. Her apartment was a fifteen minute walk away and the pop up game was ten minutes in the other direction.

Zoe practically skipped the whole way and knew she got a few weird looks from the broad grin on her face. Too freaking bad, this was going to be *awesome.*

The address was in the husk of a failed froyo shop

that Zoe had been meaning to go to but hadn't. The walls were now painted a bright white and the company had thrown up some interior walls so the only thing she could see when she entered was a white table with a frowning college student in all black scrolling through his phone.

The student silently shoved a clipboard at her. "Fill out the waiver," he said, voice monotone.

There was something... off... about the kid. Then she chastised herself for thinking that. He looked like any undergrad she might see on campus. Yeah, the goth look was kind of outdated, but so what? It was his style.

Zoe turned her attention to the waiver and her eyebrows shot up. Ten pages? And why was the font so tiny? She started to skim it, but her vision blurred. The first page seemed completely normal once she could force herself to focus, so Zoe assumed the rest of it would be as well. She scribbled her name and initials where she was supposed to and handed the form back to the kid.

Kid. Ha! As if she wasn't only twenty-five. But the last three years had been roughly a lifetime long, and some days Zoe felt like she was twenty-five going on seventy.

"Zoe Gershwin," the guy behind the counter said in his monotone. "Your match has been found. Please proceed through the door and sit in station three. It will briefly go dark. You have nothing to fear."

"Can you tell me how this game works?" She was excited to get started, sure, but usually these escape rooms or whatever had some starting guidelines. She didn't love when a game dropped her in the middle of everything and expected her to figure things out without a tutorial.

"Proceed to door three," the guy repeated.

Something was off about this place. He hadn't asked for a credit card or told her the price. There were no prices listed and no posters or art to advertise the different worlds they could offer with whatever tech they were using. There wasn't even a company name listed.

Zoe glanced back towards the door, but the windows were frosted from the inside and she couldn't make anything out.

"Would you care for a refreshment?" The guy stood from behind the desk and bent over before reappearing with a water bottle in hand.

"No, I'm good. Thanks." For some reason, she didn't walk out, even if her instincts were screaming at her. She'd always been just a bit too curious, and that wasn't stopping now.

Zoe headed in back, and the walls were just as white and barren as they were in the front. The only decorations were the numbers on the doors. She was tempted to peek past door one or two, but when she tried the handle for door one, it was locked.

Door three was cracked open. And when she saw the machine inside, she let out a breath of relief. They might be calling this high-tech, but it looked really similar to other virtual reality simulators she'd tried in the past, though a bit smaller.

As she approached, a hatch opened with a quiet hiss and revealed what appeared to be a massage chair. There were steps up into the machine, but Zoe didn't think her bag would fit. She looked around for a locker, but there wasn't one.

She placed it against the wall in front of the machine and hoped the door would remain locked while the game was going. Now that she was looking at the simulator, excitement burbled.

This was going to be so freaking cool.

She climbed in and situated herself. The chair seemed to mold around her, soft fabric curling around her calves and forearms and holding her in place while the hatch slowly closed in front of her.

It was pitch black. All Zoe could hear was her breath and the beating of her own heart.

She looked straight ahead and waited for the screen to light up, and wondered how the controls would work. She didn't feel anything under her fingers, but hopefully it would all make sense soon.

Her eyes slipped shut and she could feel herself falling and falling, her head spinning and body weightless until she jerked and opened her eyes.

It was bright.

How?

She stood up.

Where?

Zoe crouched and felt the moisture of the grass under her fingertips.

How?

If she didn't know any better, she'd say she'd been magically transported to some far off garden an unknowable distance from home. The only hint that she wasn't outside was that the air had a faintly recycled scent.

However they were doing this, the game was *awesome.* And she hadn't even started yet.

Zoe took a few steps, trying to get a sense of the controls. Walking just felt like walking. She plucked up a bit of the grass and it was as easy as ever. She tried to call up some kind of control screen to figure out how many items she could hold, but nothing appeared.

Maybe since the game was so realistic, she could only carry things in her pockets or a bag. Too bad she'd left her backpack outside the simulator.

"Hey!" a feminine voice called from behind her.

Zoe whipped around. The woman had an ephemeral quality to her, like her skin was lit from the inside by a faintly orange fire. She had short cropped dark hair that was held back by a bright red headband and wore a utilitarian jumpsuit full of enough pockets and zippers to carry any items Zoe might need.

Was she supposed to attack this woman and take her clothes?

No. That seemed like a really violent start, and Zoe didn't have any weapons.

"Hey!" the woman demanded again. "Who are you? No one's authorized to be in the Verdant Sector at this hour."

"Oh, I didn't realize that. Is this the Verdant Sector?" Maybe this was the tutorial, and if Zoe completed it correctly she'd get one of those jumpsuits of her own.

The woman gave her a confused look and grabbed a small tablet out of one of the large pockets on her leg. Light emanated like the woman was looking at a holograph, but Zoe couldn't make it out from her angle.

"Come with me," said the woman. "The administrator will sort this out."

Hmm, to go or not to go?

The woman was looking at her expectantly. Seriously, the graphics on this thing were amazing. How much rendering power was it taking to make this look so lifelike? There wasn't even a hint of the uncanny valley, even with the woman's faint glow.

Zoe followed her and hoped she'd get a tutorial inside.

But the woman wasn't interested in talking. She led Zoe down a dark, narrow hall and opened a door, gesturing for Zoe to go in.

"Stay here," the woman said once Zoe had entered. The woman stayed on the other side of the doorway. "Asher will figure out what to do with you." A breath later, the door slid closed.

Zoe rushed at it, as if she might stop it, but she just ran into solid metal.

How the hell were they doing this?

She caressed the door for a minute, the tactile sensation almost too real for her to comprehend. As soon as she got out of this game, she was going to demand to know everything she could, and hopefully the kid had more information about the company's tech.

But right now she was locked in a tiny room that was even smaller than her office.

How was she supposed to get out?

CHAPTER THREE

ASHER DIDN'T HAVE time for this. Lady Nova was coming back to the colony in a month and everything had to be perfect for that visit. He had a list of things that needed to be done that was as long as a transport ship and half the staff he needed to do it. For some reason, the citizen dragons of Vemion weren't interested in creating a colony out of half-terraformed sand.

Part of Asher couldn't blame them. Time outside was strictly rationed for safety reasons, and everyone worked the schedule of three people. He was probably working for six. And he dreaded to think of how much work his sister was taking on. She made sure he missed nothing, and that wasn't easy.

But whatever was waiting behind the door had

challenged her competence. Remy didn't like forcing him to handle problems when she knew the answers. This one had her stumped.

He keyed in the override code on the lock and the door slid open.

Asher stared.

The human woman had destroyed the office. The small desk had been flipped to its side and the two drawers were askew, their contents strewn across the floor. She stood on the desk and had the wooden chair in her hands, and was bashing it against the window as if the plas-glass was weak enough to be broken like that.

Remy hadn't suggested that this woman was crazy, just confused. Now Asher had to wonder if this was some sort of prank.

He didn't like pranks.

The woman turned towards him and his breath caught. She might have been crazy, but her beauty was a punch to his gut.

Her dark hair was held back, but strands were falling around her face, framing pale skin and wide, heavy-lidded dark eyes. Her shirt was askew, one side of the neck practically hanging off her shoulder, and it was a cheerful yellow that was somehow at odds with her behavior. Her pants were a light maroon.

People didn't bother to wear color like that on VMC12. The particulate matter in the air ended up making everything fade and the high powered laundry machines they used were great for cleaning clothes but terrible on delicate fabric.

Delicate. Ha! There was nothing delicate about a woman banging a chair against the window as if she were trying to break out of prison.

"Oh," said the woman, the sound a surprised puff of air. "Hello."

Hello? She'd torn the office apart and greeted him with hello? "Hello," he found himself saying back. Her demeanor was so strange it was short-circuiting his brain, and he couldn't find the anger he knew he should be feeling. "What are you doing?"

She set the chair down but didn't climb off the desk. "I think I've almost got this puzzle solved, right? I found the clues I needed and this window should pop open if I use them in the right order." She spoke as if those words made any kind of sense.

"That's plas-glas, nothing short of a las cannon will touch it. What puzzle?" He had to be dreaming. He'd fallen asleep at his desk while waiting for a message from the matchmaker, that was the only way this made sense.

Yet it felt like he was awake. His dreams were never so bizarre.

She scrunched up her face and pursed her lips. "The puzzle to get out of here. Where is *here,* anyway? You should definitely have some more character orientation stuff if you're just going to dump people in the middle of the game."

This had to be a prank. And Asher would get Remy back good when he had time. Or make her clean out the toilets by herself for a week. But something about this whole thing intrigued him, and he didn't walk away. "What's your name?"

The woman blinked a few times and cocked her head to the side. "Should I be making up a character?" she muttered, as if he wasn't standing right there. "Ugh, there really needs to be a tutorial." Then she shook her head and turned back to him with a smile. "I'm Zoe Gershwin. Real names are fine, I guess."

She needed to get to medical. Perhaps the doctor could tell him if something was wrong with her. Or Remy would burst out laughing and give away the prank.

"Alright, Zoe Gershwin, what were you doing in the Verdant Sector during off hours?" They had to close the sector when the terraforming machines got close enough to affect the outdoor air quality, and everyone in the compound knew that. "And which work crew are you on?"

"Do you have a name?" she asked instead of answering. "I guess I can just call you Serious Hottie Guy." She laughed to herself and looked at him as if that was some sort of normal thing to say to a person.

She found him attractive? Asher refused to preen. He knew he looked good. He'd spent a social season or two in Vemion and had his fair share of interest. "My name is Asher, I'm the administrator for VMC12." Though he didn't understand how that fact could pass her by. He was wearing his administrator's uniform with the red banding on his shoulders that indicated he was in charge. He didn't expect everyone to have his face memorized, but the banding was a universal sign.

"Asher, got it. What's VMC12? That's where we are?" She carefully climbed down from the desk but didn't try to approach him.

"How did you get here?" Access to the colony had to be tightly controlled. They only had so much food and so many medical supplies. There was no extra to provide... tourists.

Though she was the strangest tourist he'd ever seen.

Zoe stared at him and then turned away and tried to walk around him to leave the room.

He jumped in her path, both arms in front of him. "Where do you think you're going?"

"Damn it," she said to herself. "I hoped that would work. How do I get out of here?"

"You answer my questions." She really needed that medical eval. Remy could play jokes, but this went beyond anything that was in the realm of funny. There was something deeply disturbed about this woman.

She sighed and shrugged. "Alright, I guess. I woke up outside, I don't know how I got here, and then I met that woman. That's all I've got. Sorry."

Asher couldn't deal with this, not when he was already behind schedule thanks to last week's trip to Vemion. "Please don't destroy this office. Someone will be back to take care of you shortly." He backed out of the room and engaged the lock.

Whatever was going on, Remy could handle her.

Asher smelled the faintest hint of smoke as he marched through the hallway to his private quarters and knew it was wafting off him, a sure sign of draconic frustration. Once he was alone in his room, he took a moment to calm down, using the same techniques that had kept him from lashing out at his brothers when he was a child. Once his frustrations were buried deep enough to be forgotten, he opened his eyes.

His room was small and spotless. As lord-governor, he'd have an entire mansion to himself. As lead administrator, his main perk was a private bathing room and a small nook where he could get work done away from his public office.

He sent a note to Remy to have her run Zoe's name and vital information through their system to see if they could learn more about her. Once that was done, they'd have the doc check her out. Nothing about her made sense. People didn't act that way, not even when they were suffering mental affliction. It was as if she was living in a completely different world than him.

Humans weren't incredibly common on Vemion or the other dragon colonies, but there were some. Several of his cousins were mated to humans, as a matter of fact. He knew the human home planet of Earth was not wise to the expansiveness and life outside of their small solar system, but humans had been abducted from their home and spread all across the galaxy over the millennia. Zoe must have been one of them, otherwise she would have been too shocked by being on another planet to act as she did.

If she realized she was on another planet.

She was a puzzle, one parts of his mind were eager to solve. But Asher had no time for interesting women and the problems they caused.

He checked his messages again, but there was nothing from Shade. Could the matchmaker not find one dragon ready to be his bride?

His comm screen lit up with an incoming call and he tried not to be disappointed when he saw it was Lady Nova. She'd put him in charge of getting this place ready, and she'd trusted him more than anyone else ever had. He had to impress her. He took another calming breath before he engaged the call.

"Ma'am, it's good to hear from you," he answered with a polite smile.

Lady Nova was a woman in her sixties who had the energy of a twenty year old and the exacting standards of a decorated general. She was sister to the king and terrifying in her own right. She was also his cousin somehow, though the family tree was convoluted enough that he didn't feel like untangling it.

He expected her to want a report on the progress before her visit next month, but that wasn't what she spoke of. "I have a report you went to Vemion last week."

So his movements were being monitored. Lovely. "Yes, ma'am, just for two days."

She nodded and confirmed she knew exactly what he'd been doing. "To meet the matchmaker. I'm glad you took my suggestion."

Suggestion? At the time it had felt like an order. He wasn't stupid enough to say that. "It is time I found a bride, one who—"

"Is worthy of your position, of course. If only my sons were so dutiful. They've—" Lady Nova took a deep breath and forced a smile. "I'm sure you will find a wonderful wife, one who will stand behind you once you have earned your new position. I have spoken to my brother about you, you know."

"Thank you, ma'am. Your confidence is—"

She waved his words away. "Yes, yes. Now tell me about the breakdown of the thresher in the Outer Bounds. Will it delay things?"

"No, ma'am." Asher was thankful to turn the conversation to a report about terraforming and let himself sink into his roll.

But by the time the call was done, he was still thinking about the human woman in the holding room. How had she gotten here?

And why did she set his body on fire?

CHAPTER FOUR

THIS GAME MADE NO SENSE. Zoe had no idea of her objective, and the Asher character was an unfun stick in the mud who wasn't even a proper boss she could battle. Not that she had anything to battle with. Shouldn't she have acquired some items by now?

And how long had this game been going on for? It felt like she'd been playing for hours and her stomach rumbled in agreement. She hadn't eaten dinner before stepping into the VR machine.

Pizza. She was definitely picking up pizza on the way home.

"I could really use a hint!" she called out, on the faint hope that someone working the machines would hear her. She didn't know how to quit the game—definitely an oversight—but she wasn't giving up yet.

A moment later, and possibly summoned by her plea, the door opened again and the same woman who'd found her outside stood there. She wasn't as glowy now, so that might have been a trick of the light. But there was still an ethereal quality to her that made Zoe feel frumpy by comparison.

"Hello, Miss Gershwin, my name is Remy and Asher has asked me to assist you. Please hold out your hand." Remy spoke swiftly, with a tone of quiet confidence.

Zoe held out her hand before she realized she was following the order. Remy held a small scanner over it and a bright light flashed. It was warm, but not painful. A moment later, the light went dark and Remy slid the scanner into a pocket of her dark jump-suit. "What's that?" Zoe asked.

"An identity scan. Please follow me, I've prepared sleeping quarters for you." Without waiting for more questions, Remy turned and strode away.

Zoe had to jump over the forgotten chair to follow. She waited for Remy to offer more information, to perhaps give her some clues for this mission, but she said nothing.

Okay. Maybe it was up to Zoe to find out herself. Really, this game could use some guides. Did they know anything about design and flow? She was going to have *a lot* of notes on the review questionnaire at the end.

"What's VMC12? And where is everyone else? Is there some kind of... trouble?" There had to be a problem for her to fix, something that would lead to the level ending.

Remy came to a stop before a door and gestured for Zoe to raise her palm to a discreet reader. It scanned her and the door slid open.

"We are on VMC12," Remy answered. "It's the twelfth colony of Vemion and will be renamed once migration begins. No one is wandering the halls because they are busy working, and what kind of trouble could there be? I'm not sure what you're up to, but I will find out."

"I'm not up to anything." Zoe tried to imagine how Star Commander Xira would handle this, but she wasn't her favorite heroine and could only approach this as herself. There was no changing her character now when she was in the middle of the game.

Remy made a humming noise in the back of her throat. Zoe wasn't sure if that was a good or bad thing. "You may remain in your quarters, use the bathing suite down the hall, and get food in the cafeteria. Stay inside except during scheduled time in the Verdant Sector. You may explore the sector when the light above the exterior door is blue. If the light is not blue, stay inside unless it's an emergency. If you venture outside, remain in the Verdant Sector, it's dangerous to go beyond. I need your word of honor that you'll follow these rules."

"You're not locking me up?" Not that Zoe wanted to be a prisoner, but now at least she was getting a few game clues.

"You are a mystery, but I will not treat you as a criminal until you show yourself as one. We do not have the personnel to waste on guard duty for mysterious women. Now, your word?" Remy looked at her expectantly.

"Uh, yeah, sure." Easy enough to lie.

But it satisfied Remy. "Dinner service begins in two hours. If you have questions, you may send me a message on your comm screen." She pointed into the room at a black panel on the gray walls. "Do you have any questions?"

Only a million, but Zoe shook her head. "I'm good, thanks."

Remy pulled out the scanner that she'd used earlier and examined the screen, her brow furrowed.

"Is anything wrong?" asked Zoe.

"No. I'll see you later." Remy left the room and closed the door behind her.

The room was nothing special. And it was freaking tiny. Smaller than her dorm in college and only a breath or two bigger than her office. There was a bed that flipped down from the wall and a small mirror hanging on the door of a minuscule closet that proved to be empty.

She wasted a bit of time touching everything. She couldn't get over just how tactile this game was. Even with the lackluster story direction, the gameplay was neat. But she didn't want to waste any more time feeling surfaces when there was a game to play.

Remy had finally given her the clues she needed.

If the only place she wasn't supposed to go was outside, obviously that was where she was meant to be. There had to be some sort of obstacle out there for her to discover, some sort of problem to solve.

Still, Zoe waited another couple of minutes to give Remy time to leave the hallway. No use getting caught immediately. She'd have to be sneaky, they already suspected her. But at least there were no guards to worry about. So far this didn't seem to be a violent game. Zoe was more used to blasters and evil aliens, but she could appreciate a complex puzzle.

If there were an appropriate amount of clues.

Satisfied that Remy would be gone, Zoe slipped out of her room and searched for an exterior door. She found one just past the bathing suite, the light over it a forbidding yellow.

Zoe let her hand hover over the sensor for a second. Was there going to be an alarm? Should she be sneakier or maybe wait until the light turned blue?

No. The game had been clear. The clues would be in the Verdant Sector when no one else was out there, so Zoe had to go now.

She took a deep breath and opened the door, braced to hear a warning siren. But nothing sounded. Yes!

The door slid shut behind her and she started walking. Getting further from the building would be the smart thing to do, just in case there were perimeter guards or security cameras.

The Verdant Sector was everything it promised to be... green. Thick bushes and trees ringed small sitting areas, and she spotted more than one fountain burbling happily. With no one outside, the place was eerie.

Zoe followed a stone path and wondered what the thumping hum was that she heard in the distance. The air was a bit thick and something tickled the back of her throat.

How was the VR machine doing that? For real.

Was it possible this wasn't a game?

She thunked down onto a stone bench and pondered the thought, the impossibility of *that* warring with the super-real experience all around her. If she hadn't climbed into a VR machine with the intention of playing some new sci-fi game, she... well, she wouldn't know what to think.

Had she been abducted by aliens or something?

The absurdity of the thought startled a laugh out of her. Right. Aliens. A hyper realistic VR machine was *way* more feasible than freaking aliens. She'd spent her entire academic career peering at the stars in the vain hope she might find life out there some day, but this was beyond ridiculous.

"I think I'm ready to be done now." This game was weird and didn't have a plot, and whatever they were doing to her was really messing with her sinuses. But the game didn't respond to her wish.

Zoe raised her hands to her face, trying to feel for some kind of headset, but ever since she'd woken up here she hadn't felt a hint of the machine she was in. It had to be a trick. There had to be a way out. She closed her eyes and took a deep breath, ignoring the thick air. She reached out in front of herself, hoping to feel controls.

Nothing.

Damn it. What the hell was going on?

"Seriously, I quit!" She was louder this time, but nothing about her surroundings changed.

For the first time, Zoe started to feel worried. She chose to play the game. What fun was it if she was forced?

Nothing happened. The game went on around her as if she wasn't there. What happened if she couldn't get out? Would she die in here?

Her stomach rumbled again, a reminder that she hadn't eaten in awhile.

Why could she feel *that*, but nothing else about her body? Zoe couldn't face the possibility that the things around her were real. It didn't make any sense. At worst she'd somehow been abducted to some weird park outside the city. There was nothing here that screamed outer space.

Okay. Maybe she was experiencing something, and maybe it was sort of real. That's why the game wouldn't end. So she just had to find a way out of here.

Something scampered over her foot, and Zoe jumped up off the bench and looked around wildly for a rat. Instead she saw a...

Cat?

A lizard?

The creature stared at her with big eyes and

strange green scales that ended in gray fur. It chirped and then took a cautious step forward.

There definitely weren't cat lizards on Earth. And she couldn't think of a single cat that would deign to wear a costume like that. But bio-engineering was a thing. She could still be... somewhere.

The cat-lizard took a few steps and then looked back at her, as if it wanted her to follow.

Was this the game? Was she in the middle of discovering some kind of creature? Whichever it was, Zoe followed.

The cat-lizard pranced off the path and she quickly lost her bearings. But it wasn't long before the greenery coalesced into a dense wall and she spotted the outline of a door.

Yes! She was one step closer to home.

Out of a sense of thanks, Zoe reached down to pet the cat-lizard as she opened the door. Instead of accepting the affection, the damned thing swiped a gouge in her arm and darted out of the door with a hiss.

She clamped a hand on her arm to stop the bleeding. The pain was sharp and burning, and there was no way in hell this was a game. She was bleeding actual blood.

Hopefully home wasn't too far away.

But outside the door, the terrain transformed from a lush garden to a barren desert. It stretched all the way out to a mountain range in the distance. She spotted some strange... plane... possibly flying that way, but it moved like a bird... if pterodactyls still existed.

That had to be a trick of the light. Maybe it was just a really big eagle.

She skirted the edge of the wall and hoped she'd find a parking lot or something that would give her a clue of where she was. She was beyond sick of this game and wanted to go home.

The distant hum she'd heard inside the Verdant Sector grew louder. Could it be train tracks? It didn't sound exactly right, but she was getting desperate.

Zoe headed towards it, even as her survival instincts screamed at her to stay away.

Dust was so thick in the air she couldn't see more than twenty feet in front of herself, and sound travelled strangely.

Then a dark shadow the size of a building rose up in front of her and Zoe had to bite back a scream. She stumbled back and tripped over her own feet. And by the time she scrambled back up, the machine was closer and moving impossibly fast.

What was it?

No time to worry about that.

She ran like a bear was chasing her, but no matter how fast she pumped her legs, the shadow of the machine grew larger. There was no outrunning it, and it was too big to dodge around.

Was this how it ended? Crushed by a mystery machine in the middle of a weird-ass abduction?

A different shadow crossed over head, and Zoe looked up just in time to see a giant dragon diving over her, claws out and headed straight for her.

She screamed and dove to the ground, covering her head as best she could.

CHAPTER FIVE

THE HUMAN HAD A DEATH WISH. The certainty of that fact rang through Asher's mind as he rushed her to the medical station in the compound. No one else would be foolish enough to leave the safety of the Verdant Sector and stare down a terraforming thresher.

Two utility crew members jumped out of his way as he swung around a corner, and he nearly plowed over a lunch cart and the cafeteria staff member pushing it. Asher ignored them. He had to get Zoe to the doctor.

She'd lost consciousness the second he grabbed her in his claws, and he was concerned he might have hurt her in his hurry to save her. The moment the breach warning had sounded, everything in him had known that it was her and Asher had taken off. It didn't matter that there were staff members responsible for retrieving anyone who ended up outside the Verdant Sector.

Asher had to save her.

It didn't make sense. He wasn't a foolish man and neither was he impulsive, but something deep inside of him had demanded that he take off and find the troublesome human before something bad happened to her.

But she wouldn't wake up.

His heartbeat pounded wildly, sweat beaded on his brow, and he knew his expression had to be forbidding. If anyone dared approach him right now, he would... well, he wasn't quite sure what he'd do, but it would not be kind.

He shouldered his way into the medical center and glared at the medbot that handled the most common scrapes and bruises. He wanted a person seeing to Zoe, not a hunk of wires and metal.

The medbot tried to intercept him, but Asher danced around it and proceeded through the door back to Cirk's office. The doctor jumped out of his chair when he spotted Asher, his face going red and a puff of angry smoke haloing his head for a moment before it dissipated.

He opened his mouth to say something, but then

he noticed the unconscious woman in Asher's arms. "What did you do?"

Anyone else who took that tone with him would be out of a job and on the first ship back to Vemion. But the doctor understood just how vital his position was, and he wasn't afraid to stand up to Asher. Asher gently lay Zoe down on the examination table, his fingers gliding down her arm before he forced himself to take a step back. "She left the Verdant Sector. I grabbed her in my claws before a thresher could get to her, it was less than ten meters away. She lost consciousness immediately. She's human," he added, as if it needed to be said.

Humans and dragons looked similar on the surface, though most dragons had a faint, scale-like pattern to their skin in their human forms. The thing that truly separated them was the shifting. Asher couldn't imagine being bound to one form for his entire life, to never feel the air under his wings or the fire on his breath.

Cirk's demeanor shifted from affronted to intent between one breath and the next. "We don't get many humans out here."

No, they didn't. The human population of Vemion and its colonies numbered in the hundreds or, perhaps, the low thousands. As far as Asher could remember, they didn't have any humans on permanent staff, and it was possible that Zoe was the only human on the planet.

"Can you treat her?" he demanded. "What's wrong?" He wasn't touching her anymore, but he couldn't make himself step back any further. An insane part of himself wanted to jump in front of the doctor, as if Zoe needed to be protected from him.

Something was messing with Asher. He didn't have time to think about it.

Cirk grabbed a scanner and ran it over Zoe, watching the small screen intently. He hummed in the back of his throat and pursed his lips before grabbing a second scanner and repeating the process.

"What is it?" Asher wanted to grab him by the collar and shake him.

Cirk looked up, startled, as if he'd forgotten Asher was there in the two minutes it had taken to scan the human. "Why are you still here? Get out and let me work."

"What. Is. Wrong?" He ground the words out between clenched teeth.

The doctor, bastard that he was, gave a casual shrug. "I'm not sure yet. Her vitals don't concern me at the moment. I'll need to run some more scans. I'll send you an update once I know more. Go do your job, my lord, and let me do mine." He met Asher's gaze with the calm certainty of a man used to being obeyed.

Asher could make this a battle. Cirk was king of his little medical kingdom, but Asher was still in charge. But Cirk was the only one who could help Zoe. Asher relented. "I want updates on the hour and to know the moment she wakes up." He left before Cirk could make a remark about that command.

When he was back in the hall, he could feel eyes on him. Many of his staff were headed towards the cafeteria for lunch, and they seemed to be idling in the hall more than usual. One of the dragons that Asher was almost certain was on the road construction crew met his eyes and then grinned. He opened his mouth as if he was about to make a joke, and Asher glared.

The crewman snapped his mouth shut and lowered his gaze.

Good.

Asher stalked back to his office, and whatever the whispers were, none of them reached his ears. He couldn't bring himself to care, not when half his mind was stuck back in medical quarters and worrying about Zoe.

Who was she? How was she here?

What in all of the stars had provoked her to leave

the relatively safety of the Verdant Sector when the threshers were so close?

He pulled up the security feed and rewound it to when it had picked up her presence. He scowled as she bent down to address one of the lizard-cats that had managed to get into the Verdant Sectors. Those pests were going to overrun the place if he didn't do something about it.

And then he watched in disbelief as she just... followed the animal out of the Verdant Sector and through a door to the untamed wilds of VMC12.

She really did have a death wish. Or she'd been born without sense.

His comm beeped with a terse message from the doctor. *I gave her a sedative. She'll wake in the morning.*

That was it. No explanation for her unconsciousness. Nothing.

Asher almost wrote back demanding a more detailed report, but he forced himself to calm down. This wasn't like him. He cared about this place and the people he was responsible for, but he didn't go chasing after idiots who tried to get themselves killed. He didn't hover over people in the infirmary, helpless as his mind conjured up every misfortune that could befall them.

He didn't know this woman. Remy still hadn't

handed over whatever data she'd managed to gather, so he was flying blind.

It was the mystery of her, that was all. He tried to convince himself of that as he checked his morning calendar and moved around a few meetings to open up his schedule.

And still nothing from Shade. How was he supposed to claim a bride if the matchmaker wouldn't contact him?

His communicator buzzed with an incoming message and he jumped to check it, fearing a sudden turn in Zoe's condition. Instead, it was the same matchmaker he'd just been mentally questioning. Maybe the rumors about her psychic powers were true.

Lord Asher,

I have been unable to locate a woman who fits your requirements and is currently located on VMC12. Please inform me of your next scheduled visit to Vemion and I shall set up a meeting with a proper potential bride.

If you are willing to broaden your search criteria, I may have someone perfect for you on your colony.

I look forward to your response.

Shade

Matchmaker, IDA

He wished she'd sent him a paper letter if only so

he could crumple it in a fist and throw it out. He wasn't asking for much, though he wished he could say he was surprised. He knew every soul on VMC12. The women here were hard workers and dedicated to the cause. But they weren't bride material, at least not for him.

He slumped back in his seat and groaned. Remy, having the extra senses granted to all younger sisters, chose that moment to walk in. She sank into the seat in front of his desk and waited for him to speak.

"The matchmaker wants me to go back to Vemion." It wasn't the most important thing. It wasn't even the thing he cared about the most. But it was freshest in his mind.

Remy made an undignified sound. "I told you it was a waste of time."

He glared and set his communicator face down on the desk, hiding the message from sight rather than deleting it. "What have you found out about her?" There was no need to specify *who*.

Remy threw her hands up and shrugged. "Not a clue. Zoe Gershwin, human, doesn't show up in any of our databases. Her biometric data isn't flagged anywhere. There were no incoming or outgoing ships scheduled for this morning, so she couldn't have come in that way. The cameras in the Verdant Sector malfunctioned in the quadrant where she was discovered for about an hour, you'll never guess when."

"I think I can." The picture his sister painted wasn't a good one.

"And now half the compound thinks the human is who you're taking for a bride and that she fell off you during a flight gone wrong—what?" She stopped talking and Asher realized he was standing.

He didn't mean to, he had nowhere else to go at the moment, but... what? "My bride?" He managed to keep his tone even, almost pleasant. Anger and something he couldn't identify swirled in his gut. "Who started that rumor?"

"Not a clue," his sister replied with annoying equanimity. "You know how rumors happen here, there's no tracking them to the source. And you did run through the place with the girl clutched in your arms like some sort of hero of old. Can you blame people for making up stories?"

"Yes, when they're gossiping about me!" He forced himself to sit back down before his skin started smoking and he proved to Remy just how much it bothered him. Not the idea of making Zoe his bride, of course, but the talk.

... Of course?

Zoe Gershwin, mystery human, *wasn't* a suitable

bride. She was on the colony under mysterious circumstances and might have bad intentions. What other reason would she have for showing up? Or, given the way she'd acted when they questioned her, there was something wrong with her.

He needed to find out.

Getting close to her was the only option.

He ignored the fact that Remy was sitting right there and more than capable of doing the job. This was something that Asher knew, deep in the heart of his flame, that was his responsibility.

"Did you just come here to spread more rumors?" he asked.

"Well, I was going to give you my afternoon report, but not if you're going to light me on fire just for speaking." She leaned forward as if to stand up.

He waved her off. "Give me the report. We still have work to do."

The rest of the day dragged on. Asher listened to Remy as best he could, but his focus was split, half of him still hovering over Zoe and worried Cirk might message him at any moment with terrible news. He glared at another one of his officers in the cafeteria that evening when the man tried to sit near him and Remy had to run interference before he caused an incident.

He was acting out. This wasn't him. Still, as he walked to his quarters before bed, he swung down the hall where the infirmary was but refused to poke his head in. Zoe was fine. He'd know if she wasn't.

A sleepless night left him in an even worse mood once morning dawned. And though he had a hundred responsibilities piling up, he ordered a tray of food and took it with him to the infirmary just as the entire day shift of the compound was waking up.

Cirk's eyes flicked up and down, taking stock of him and his food tray, but the doctor stepped aside and let him into the small room where Zoe was sitting up in bed and looking out the window.

She was more subdued today. Her hair was bound back and her skin looked a bit washed out in the yellow-green medical gown the doctor had given her. Her gaze glid over to him and she swallowed heavily.

"It's not a game." The words were quiet and the blanket covering her legs moved as she shifted. "I have no idea what's going on, but it's real."

He didn't understand what she was saying, so he placed the breakfast tray on the rolling table beside her bed and poured her some tea. "Are you hungry?"

"Will I be stuck in the underworld if I eat?" she asked, then groaned. "I'm sorry, I think I'm losing my grip on reality."

"This isn't the underworld." He handed the tea over and one of the fluffy biscuits slathered in butter. The compound's baker made miracles with the limited ingredients she had. With any other person, Asher would have been withholding food until he had answers. But Zoe summoned up something gentle within him. He wanted to feed her, to make sure she was safe, and to banish that terrified shadow from her eyes. He plated the other biscuit for himself and took a bite, as if that proved it was safe.

It was enough for her. She scarfed down the biscuit in a few bites and then reached for the dried fruit strips. Once those were gone, she eyed the second half of his biscuit and he pushed it towards her before she tried to steal it. Finally sated, she took her teacup and sat back, sipping daintily and looking refreshed.

Asher had to tear his gaze away to stop from staring. His flame churned deep within him, straining to reach out and touch her, as if that wouldn't mean destruction and chaos. He'd never reacted this way to a person before and he needed to get control of himself before he did something he'd regret.

"Am I really on an alien planet?" Zoe asked. Then she corrected herself. "Am I really an alien on *your* planet? You're not human."

"I'm a dragon," he confirmed. "We're on a colony called VMC12 and my home planet is called Vemion, it's about a day's flight from here."

She set her teacup down, hands shaking a bit. She curled them into fists before hiding them below her blanket. "You look human." Then she leaned in closer, staring at the exposed skin of his neck. He felt her gaze like a caress. "Except..." She lifted one of those hiding hands and reached out, but pulled it away before she touched him. "There's a faint pattern on your skin."

His throat bobbed as he swallowed hard, and he clenched every muscle in his body to keep himself under control. They were in the infirmary. She'd spent the night sedated. She had no idea where she was or what was going on. And here he was fighting off a cockstand and doing his damnedest not to fantasize about her.

"How did you get here?" The question came out sharper than intended. "You said you thought this was a game."

She sat back, nodding. "I was at home. In Nashville. That's in Tennessee, in—it's on Earth. I'm doing my PhD in astrophysics and I love virtual reality games." She looked at him expectantly, but he didn't interrupt. She continued. "I got invited to test out this new game and I went. I climbed into this machine and everything went black for a second. Then the lights came back and I was... here? I guess. How? I—" She paused for a moment and squeezed her eyes shut.

Asher saw a hint of tears. He wanted to reach out and wipe them away. Instead he held onto his teacup like it was a life preserver.

"I thought I was in some extremely advanced virtual reality world. That's why I, oh god, I could have died." Her breath rushed out of her and she sobbed, but no tears fell, and after a moment she recovered. "That's why I was acting so *stupid*. I thought they were puzzles in the game, problems I had to solve. Instead I'm somehow living out my greatest freaking dream by being on another planet and discovering that aliens actually exist and I think I'm going to throw up." She turned to her side, but after a few more heaving sobs, her breathing evened out and she didn't vomit.

Thankfully.

Asher couldn't stop himself from reaching out and taking her hand. Her skin was smooth under his and she gripped onto him, surprisingly strong. "Your greatest dream?"

She left her hand in his as she sat back up and smiled shakily. "It's why I decided to study an atrociously difficult degree. I wanted to find alien life on some far off planet. I also wanted to be an astronaut, but figured out that would never happen. And here I am. Somehow. Where is here, exactly?"

He found himself smiling and slid his chair a bit closer. "I'm afraid I don't have a celestial map handy."

"Do you have any idea how I got here?" Her gaze was completely open, as if she thought he had all the answers.

It was a heady thing. But Asher forced himself to think. "Teleportation, perhaps. It's risky over long distances, but some claim to have mastered it. You might have been put into stasis on a ship and then been teleported here once you were in range. We have no record of a ship arriving when you appeared." He probably shouldn't be telling her those details. This whole fantastical story might be a concoction made up so she could finagle her way inside and learn their secrets or sabotage the colony.

Then again, if he were sending in saboteurs, he'd give them believable stories. He believed every word Zoe said, even if he didn't quite understand half of them, but that didn't make her story any less ludicrous.

"How can I understand you?" she asked. "You're not speaking English, right? And I only speak a bit of

Spanish, so it's not like I magically learned a new language."

He held up a hand, reaching out, and paused before he touched her. "May I?"

She nodded.

He gently pressed the skin behind her ear, feeling for the tell-tale bumps of a subdermal translator. There was no real need to touch her, but he savored the feel of her soft skin under his fingertips and sucked in a harsh breath when she nuzzled into his palm. He could sit like that forever, but Asher forced himself to pull away.

Zoe stared at him, dark eyes wide and cheeks flushed.

He had to wet his lips before he spoke, mouth suddenly dry. "Someone placed a translator behind your ear. They recognize and process most known languages and can learn undiscovered languages when given sufficient data."

She traced a finger behind her ear. "That doesn't feel like anything. Where does it store the processing power? Has it integrated with my brain? Is it safe?"

He could only answer the last question. "Perfectly safe, I've had one for years. I don't know the rest, just that it works. I could have Cirk—that's the doctor—remove yours if it would make you more comfortable."

It was only right to make the offer, but Asher didn't want to lose the ability to communicate.

She shook her head. "Maybe before I go home. *Can I go home?* If I've travelled light years away…"

"We'll find a way. I think our technology might surprise you." His comm beeped, alerting him that he had other places to be. Asher wanted to ignore it to spend more time with Zoe and unravel her secrets… and maybe to find an excuse to touch her again. Instead, he stood. "Cirk will give you some less… colorful clothes in a bit and you will be released from the infirmary. Please don't leave the Verdant Sector again."

She shook her head and held her hands up, palms facing out. "Scout's honor, I don't want to do that again."

He had to leave her there, then. Cirk gave him a knowing look as he passed, but Asher ignored him. He'd have to figure out what to do with Zoe and soon, but the thought of sending her home made everything inside of him rebel.

There was a message waiting for him when he got back to his desk. It was from Lady Nova.

I hear you've found a human bride. I look forward to meeting her.

CHAPTER SIX

Zoe was an idiot a million times over. She was about to burst out of her skin from the shame of it and wished she could do yesterday over. Maybe then she wouldn't run headfirst into danger on the reckless notion that she was invincible and in a video game.

Ha!

She'd *known* it couldn't be real. How many VR games had she played? Fifty? More? They were never really real, no matter how good the graphics. Nothing could trick the mind for long. And yet she'd been walking around as if she truly believed someone had found the trick to doing it without inducing terrible nausea and headaches.

And even now it was still easier to believe she was trapped inside some super advanced VR game instead of on an alien planet. She'd just have everything she ever dreamed of proven true. Aliens were real! There were other inhabited planets! Advanced space travel existed.

She was the furthest a human had ever been from Earth.

Maybe.

Zoe slumped down onto the bed in the small quarters she'd been given and turned that idea around in her head. *Was* she the only human not on Earth? Asher sure hadn't seemed shocked by her species. And with humans and dragons looking so similar, did that suggest a common ancestor? Or was there something in the primordial space mists that tended towards human shapes?

Her room was tiny. It held a narrow bed and a small wardrobe filled with utilitarian clothing ranging in color from dark gray to lighter gray. There was an even narrower window that let in a bit of sunlight, but the glass was frosted so she couldn't see outside.

It felt a little bit like a prison cell. Frankly, Zoe was lucky she wasn't locked up. She'd even tested it right after being released from the infirmary. The door slid open under her command. No one had challenged her as she'd walked to the cafeteria and back.

Asher was giving her a second chance.

A small smile tugged at her lips and she had to force it off her face. Just because the super sexy man-dragon had given her a bit of attention and was understanding about her predicament didn't mean she was going to let her tummy go all wobbly over the guy. She couldn't find a decent boyfriend back on Earth, what made her think an alien would want her?

She was getting way ahead of herself.

She didn't need a space boyfriend. What she needed was a ride back home. Sure, her childhood dream had been to be some sort of space explorer like a mix of Captain Kirk and Princess Leia. But Zoe had a life back home.

Had anyone even noticed she was gone?

How long *had* she been gone?

The distances were hard to fathom, especially given that this was what she studied. She knew just how big space was and just how impossible faster than light travel was. If things were still bound by the laws of physics as she knew them, then there might not be any going back home. It might have been decades—even centuries—since she left in the first place.

Now her stomach wobbled and it had nothing to do with sexy dragon dudes.

The walls were closing in on her. Her breaths came in too fast and sweat popped up on her arms.

Zoe shot up off the bed. She had to get out of here before she curled into a ball and gave up.

The door opened when she pressed the button on the control panel and no one was in the hall outside. She took the exact same path she'd taken yesterday and found the door into the Verdant Sector. Now the light above it indicated that it was safe to go outside. Good. Zoe didn't know what she would have done if she couldn't get fresh air.

As soon as she was through the door and in the open area, some of the tension in her chest began to ease and the queasiness faded.

She looked at the Verdant Sector with new eyes. The day before she'd been determined to find clues in a fake game, looking for her next step rather than appreciating the place for what it was. Today she just walked.

Deep green vines grew up walls and sculptures throughout the place, and from in the vines, flowers flourished. The whole place was kind of humid and the air smelled like she was deep in a forest, even if the sky overhead was open and cloudless. It was peaceful out here and she was surprised that no one else was taking it in.

Then again, other people had jobs. She wasn't sure what went into terraforming a planet, but it looked like a lot. Should she be asking if she could help out?

No. She should be hunting down Asher and finding a way to get home. If there was still a home to go to.

But she couldn't force herself to turn around and make her demands just yet. Exploration was her long-held fantasy. Going home meant saying goodbye to all of this and never speaking of it again. She couldn't exactly say she'd been abducted by aliens and expect to have a career when it was all over.

Sure, she knew of professors who staunchly believed in aliens. But they kept those thoughts for after hours.

Zoe wasn't sure this was something she could forget. Ever. And maybe it was a good thing she didn't have many friends. There was no one to tell.

Her mom would have listened.

She had to squeeze her eyes shut to keep the tears from falling. Grief was a bastard, and it had a way of punching a person in the gut at the absolute worst times.

But it was true. Her mom would have listened and eventually she might have believed Zoe, or at least pretended to.

Zoe would never be relieved her mother was dead, but a part of her was thankful that her mom wasn't there to miss her right now, that she couldn't be worried that Zoe had disappeared out of thin air and might never return.

Oh god, she really had to stop thinking about this.

Zoe kept moving. If she was moving she couldn't be thinking. She forced herself to pay attention to the flowers and everything around her, and she smiled when one of the strange lizard-kitties stuck its head out from under a bench.

There was no mark on her arm from the scratch she'd gotten the day before and she wasn't going to blame an animal from fleeing danger.

Zoe crouched down, bracing herself on the bench with one hand. "Hey there, little guy. What are you doing out here?"

The lizard-kitty chirped at her and blinked its wide, green eyes. Then it took a cautious step forward and bumped its head against her knee. If it had been a cat back at home, Zoe would be petting it already. Was that what it wanted?

It chirped again and rubbed against her leg.

Zoe petted it, and the chirps turned into a rumbling purr. She gave up her crouch and sat on the ground, petting the lizard-kitty for several minutes until it gave a final chirp and ran off, disappearing through some vines into another part of the Verdant Sector.

She knew she should probably wash her hands, but it could wait until she got inside.

She kept walking, trying to keep her simmering panic at bay. And once she'd smelled a few flowers and spotted a few more lizard-kitties, it was starting to work.

"I wouldn't touch that," a deep, masculine voice warned from behind her.

Zoe had been about to touch a bright orange flower that smelled like heaven. She pulled her hand back at the warning and turned around to find Asher standing there. "Why not?"

He was very handsome in the sunlight, in a buttoned up sort of way. He needed to grow his dark hair out a few inches and let it get tousled in the wind. And though he wore his uniform well, she wondered what he might look like in some old jeans and a t-shirt.

Hot.

Whatever he was wearing, he'd look hot. But the jeans might make him approachable, and then there'd be no telling what she did.

He needed to be ruffled, to have that perfectly

pressed uniform and perfectly placed hair mussed a bit. And maybe it was the craziness of the past two days talking, but she wanted to be the one to do it.

There was no doubt. Zoe had gone bonkers.

"The plant secretes an oil on its leaves. It will make you very itchy," he explained to Zoe, who had nearly forgotten what they were talking about.

She took a step away from the plant, as if it might start projecting the itchy oil at her at any second.

"Walk with me?" Asher asked.

"Of course."

Asher wound his way down the stone path, but didn't say anything. The silence was peaceful, and with his towering presence at her side, some of the nastier thoughts that had been plaguing Zoe refused to surface.

They ended up at a small, unlit firepit and sat down beside one another on the bench. She stared at the wood in the pit and tried to ignore the feel of Asher's body heat beside her.

Impossible.

She wanted to lean sideways and let him wrap an arm around her, as if this was a date and he was about to bring out the s'mores. And if she tilted her head towards him, she wouldn't be able to stop herself from leaning in and stealing a taste.

He had kissable lips. Kissable everything, really, and her body was reminding her of just how long it had been since she'd had a satisfying romp in the sheets.

Would Asher help her break her dry spell?

She'd be more than alright with his alien probe.

"Can you shoot fire?" She had to ask something before she said something even more inappropriate. "Or is that just a myth?"

Asher held up a hand in front of him, and a moment later, a ball of flame appeared.

Zoe reached out as if she could touch it, then snapped her hand back. Was she crazy? That was *fire*. Fire burned. It didn't matter what planet she was on, that was a universal constant.

Asher stared at her as if she might reach out again, and he held his hand a little behind him to keep clear of her.

Well, probably fair. She must be gaining a well-earned reputation for recklessness.

"Can you light the fire?" she asked, more than a little eager for tricks.

He shrugged and lobbed the ball of fire at the wood. It caught with a *whoosh* and the wood crackled.

"Freaking cool." It was pleasantly warm outside, and the fire could make it hot in no time, but Zoe didn't move, didn't try to put space between herself and Asher. She'd sweat out a bit of discomfort if it meant she could be close.

She might have been developing a bit of a crush, but she decided she didn't care. Everything was too weird right now for her to figure out, and a tiny crush was familiar. Sort of.

"So why'd you come find me?" she asked. They'd been sitting side by side for quite some time, and Asher still hadn't said anything.

She glanced his way and saw his throat bob as he swallowed. Then he turned fully towards her and spoke.

"I have a proposal for you."

CHAPTER SEVEN

Zoe's natural scent mixed in with the smell of the flowers all around them, a dizzying concoction. It wouldn't take any effort to reach out and touch her, to cup her cheek as he had that morning.

This time he wouldn't let her go.

His blood sang with need. His cock ached. And if he had been a different man, if they were in a different world, he might have been able to act on his wants.

But they were on VMC12 and he had a job to do. Ambitions to meet.

He stood. Sitting beside the human was far too tempting, and what he was about to say was all business, no matter what she might think.

"A proposal?" Zoe asked. She remained on the

bench, but tore her gaze away from the blazing fire to look at him.

The urge to pace was strong, but Asher clamped his hands behind his back and held still. He'd been stared down by the king on more than one occasion, this was nothing.

Yeah, right.

The idea had seemed perfect when he came up with it. He didn't have time to venture back to Vemion to find a bride, but Lady Nova expected to see one in a matter of weeks. And now, here was Zoe, fallen into his lap as if fate was smiling on him. "I need a bride."

That had her shooting off the bench and scampering back to put it between them. "What?" She held her arms out in front of her as if he might take her by force.

Asher kept himself exceedingly still, like he had to calm a wild beast. Perhaps this could have been done with a bit more finesse, but he was running out of time. "I am in search of a bride," he repeated. "Do you understand my position here?"

Zoe shook her head tightly, and her gaze was still closed off and cautious. "You're in charge."

He wished. "I'm the administrator," he corrected. "Lady Nova is the ultimate authority here, but she has taken another position that requires more of her time and trusted me in this role to see things done as she wishes."

"Okay, so you're second in command," she said. "What does that have to do with a... bride?"

She wasn't from Vemion, he reminded himself, and she didn't have decades of knowledge of the eccentricities of those in charge. "Lady Nova is a strong proponent of marriage," he explained. "Her three sons have recently wed, and she would strongly prefer to leave the running of this place in the hands of someone with a family." The fact that Lady Nova had been widowed for more than a decade and was in no rush to remarry was never to be mentioned.

"You're saying you need a wife to get a promotion." She loosened up a little, no longer braced for an attack.

"I must appear to be making the effort." Zoe didn't meet any of the criteria on his list, but he was wise enough to keep that to himself. He didn't need to marry her for this to work.

"Why me?" She tilted her head to the side and gave him a piercing look.

Hells above, she'd make a strong partner for anyone who dared to take her. But not for him, even as his body craved her.

"You're here." It was as simple as that. Mostly.

"And rumors have already started to circulate about our... relationship. Along with my recent meeting with the Intergalactic Dating Agency, people have begun to draw their own conclusions."

A strange look crossed her face, but she didn't speak.

"I would request your assistance for about a month, just through Lady Nova's next visit. I..." How could he put this lightly? "Lady Nova is a woman with very exacting standards, and a human is not likely to meet them. If she does not approve the match, there is no reason to move forward, but she will still appreciate that I've made the effort. She'll see that I'm a capable administrator and recommend me to the king for the governorship."

"Sounds nice for you. What do I get except for the wrath of a scary lady dragon and the humiliation of being dumped?" She stepped back around the bench so they no longer had that physical barrier between them, and that had to be a good sign.

Despite her frown, Asher smiled. "I'll get you passage on a luxury vessel to take you home, or anywhere else in the universe you'd like to go. And this." He reached into his pocket and pulled out a small black silk bag and handed it over to her.

Zoe took it and opened it, dipping her fingers

inside and extracting a small ruby. Her mouth dropped open, and she made a high-pitched sound in the back of her throat. "Holy hell. How many are there?"

"Do you need more?" The stones had been sitting in his quarters for nearly a year, the pouch won off of Knox in a card game. "I'm uncertain of how currency works in your world. Do gems have value?" He'd done a cursory search for information about Earth and noted that they appreciated jewels, so it was an easy way to offer payment.

"There have to be over a hundred here. Goodbye student loans." She carefully put the ruby back in the pouch and tied the strings. "You said you could send me home? Is that even possible?"

He furrowed his brow. "Why wouldn't it be?"

"Because we're *light years* away from Earth, and faster than light travel is impossible? Even if, theoretically, you could send me back to Earth, so much time will have passed that everyone I know is already dead." She squeezed her eyes shut.

Asher's heart broke, and before he could think better of it, he closed the distance between them and wrapped his arms around her. Zoe went stiff for a second and then sagged, leaning against him. He flattened a hand on her back and rubbed gently, offering what comfort he could, even if he wasn't accustomed to doing so.

No one in the compound would believe this soft side of him even if they saw it.

He didn't give a single damn.

After a moment, Zoe pulled back. "I should probably have qualms about accepting so much money," she said, but she didn't hand over the pouch.

"Why?" He had plenty more where that came from. As a dragon lord, money had never been a problem.

She shook her head and asked a different question. "How long would it take for me to get home?"

"A few days, perhaps, depending on the ship." If he had to send her away, he'd put her in the hands of someone he trusted, someone who wouldn't take advantage. Maybe he'd even escort her himself.

That was foolish. He didn't have the time. This whole plot was designed to save time, not waste a week traveling to a backwater that had no knowledge of the wider universe.

He didn't want to think of the end of this thing when it hadn't properly begun.

"Is that a yes? May I court you?" *Pretend*, he reminded himself. It was a façade to fool Lady Nova, nothing more. It had to be.

He held out his hand, hoping to seal the deal by clasping forearms.

Zoe looked down and then back up at him. "I think this is the kind of deal you seal with a kiss."

Oh, that would be unwise. His blood heated, and he couldn't tear his gaze away from her red lips. He'd imagined the taste of her more than once. And all he had to do was lean forward and there'd be no need to imagine anymore.

It was beyond foolish. But he wasn't one to deny a lady, especially one who was doing him such a huge favor.

He stepped forward. Zoe looked up.

They leaned in.

The fire at the core of him stoked into a conflagration as their lips touched, the taste of her crashing into him in one breath. It should have been a simple meeting of the lips, but her mouth opened beneath him and Asher swept inside, powerless to hold back.

She clutched him close, making a noise against him that had his blood pounding even harder, his cock twitching with need.

He wanted to lay her down on the bench and take her right there, heedless of the fact they were in the Verdant Sector where anyone could see.

Let them. With the way she fired his blood, she made him feel like a god.

It was Zoe who had the sense to pull back while his blood was still rushing. She raised a hand to her lips and their gazes locked.

He wanted to kiss her again. Wanted far more than that.

Wanted everything.

Instead he gave her a solemn nod. "I should like to dine with you tonight." Then he turned on his heel and fled.

CHAPTER EIGHT

She'd crossed half the freaking galaxy and her date was still obsessed with his phone.

Zoe snuck glances at Asher, hoping that *maybe* she'd catch his eye and knock a bit of shame into him. Sure, this was supposed to be a fake relationship, but shouldn't they be putting on a show? Wasn't her fake fiancé supposed to at least pretend to like her?

She heaved a sigh and dug into her food. It looked delicious, but there was a strange aftertaste she couldn't quite kick. Asher had explained that they relied on food processors to artificially replicate flavors, but the taste buds could never be completely fooled.

This was the third dinner she'd had with him in the roped off section of the cafeteria, and the rest of the compound's staff hadn't completely lost interest. But they weren't staring quite as much.

"If you need to go take care of something, I'd understand." Her meal was almost done, but Asher had barely touched his plate. Zoe made a mental note to mention it to Remy in the hopes that someone fed her fake-betrothed. She didn't want him to real-starve.

Asher set his device down and looked at her, blinking several times as if he had forgotten she was there. "What?"

If this was a real date, she'd be insulted by now. She tried not to take it personally and considered this her good deed for the century. She didn't want some poor, unsuspecting alien dragon woman to end up with a workaholic who couldn't even spare a minute to fake a conversation.

Not even his sexiness could make up for that.

"You've been looking at that thing for the last half hour. I know this is all..." She shrugged. They were in a mostly private area, but she didn't want to admit to the falsehood where someone might overhear. "I know you're busy."

He had the grace to look sheepish, something she didn't realize dragons could do. "I apologize. I'm being an ass."

"A little bit." She gave him a smile, hoping to soften the blow.

"How have you been finding the compound since…" He trailed off, clearly unsure of the polite way to phrase it.

"Since I stopped deluding myself that I was in a video game and accepted the totally reasonable fact that I'm halfway across the galaxy and talking to a man-dragon?" Saying it didn't make it feel any more real.

"I'm not sure it's halfway," he said before digging into his meal.

The absurdity of the thing startled a laugh out of her. But the reality had her sobering quickly. "The compound is…" She wasn't sure how to answer. Whatever the distance, she was on another freaking planet and should be soaking up the experience for all it was worth. Instead she was kind of bored. "There's not much to do here."

He wasn't offended by the admission. "We'll begin building the city once a sufficient amount of territory has—" Asher's communicator beeped and he made a face. "I'm sorry, I need to check this."

Zoe just shrugged. She picked at the rest of her food while Asher listened to the call, and it was only a couple of minutes later that he hung up. "Do you have to get back to work?" she asked. Then she wanted to smack herself. Why did she sound so disappointed? They were just putting on a show, he didn't owe her anything.

He contemplated his communicator for a minute before sliding it into his pocket, a determined look on his face. "No, not quite yet. Have you finished eating?"

She nodded. The food was strange, but at least she was well fed.

"Would you care to see the night garden?" He offered his hand.

Zoe could feel every eye in the dining hall on them. The whole room seemed to be holding its breath, as if this meant something more than she could imagine. Or maybe she was just losing it.

She placed her hand in his and stopped paying attention to anything else.

Asher led her out of the room and into the Verdant Sector, but instead of turning towards the main pathway that she'd been walking every day, he headed towards a metal wall and stopped in front of a door that she'd assumed was a utility shed.

The door slid open with a whisper, no need to unlock it or anything, and they stepped through into a world of magic.

Zoe's mouth dropped open, and she choked on a

gasp. Delicate blinking lights flickered on strings overhead, providing just enough illumination to make out the brilliant white flowers that climbed the other side of that metal wall up delicate trellises. They were mixed in with dark vines and small blooms that she feared would crumble into nothing if she touched them.

"The night garden?" She wasn't sure what she was asking. She stepped closer to the wall and paused when Asher dropped her hand, the absence sudden and unwanted.

"My mother is an ardent gardener," Asher explained. "She insisted that I give the night blooming plants a home of their own so that there's beauty at every hour in this desolate place."

"Desolate? Is that her word? Has she seen this place?" Zoe's mom would have hated it. Not the garden, of course. The Verdant Sector was gorgeous. But inside felt like the worst possible mix of an office building and a hospital.

Antiseptic.

Impersonal.

Cold.

The only thing cold about the night garden was the slight chill in the evening air, and Zoe could easily ignore that. Even the ever present hum of the terraforming machines was distant. She and Asher were in their own secret sliver of the universe.

He took a few steps closer, until he was right behind her, and reached a hand over her shoulder to pluck a large white bloom from its stem. He held it in front of Zoe until she took it for herself, savoring the rich, almost savory scent of the flower.

"Remy is my only family member who's been to VMC12. My brothers are happy to make their homes on Vemion and satisfy themselves with our family's wealth. They don't..." He sighed and then cleared his throat. "One of my brothers collects every bauble he can find. I don't think he'll be satisfied until he owns at least one of every kind of gem in the universe. The collection is beautiful, but I want to build something."

But he thought this place was desolate.

Zoe didn't press him on it. She absolutely understood not loving your job. If Asher had mixed feelings, he was hardly the only person in the universe.

"Is this place just for you?" It felt like a haven.

He shook his head. "When I'm lord-governor, perhaps I'll make a private garden. Right now the only places that are restricted are for safety reasons. No special privileges. My only luxury is larger quarters."

What kind of luxury was a larger prison cell?

The thought was enough to startle Zoe, and she

had to shake her head to dislodge it. She was seeing something no human had ever seen before. She was living her wildest fantasy. How could she think of this as prison?

Asher had chosen this life, he wasn't stuck here.

She laced their fingers together and tugged him further down the path. "Show me more flowers."

She braced herself with every step for the buzz of his communicator, but in the dim light it was silent. She didn't for a second believe that he'd left it inside, but perhaps he was making an effort.

That effort would be better made where they could be seen. This relationship was all for show, a fake courtship to consolidate his position. Nothing more.

She could forget all that under the night sky. Asher's fingers were warm under hers. He was a solid presence beside her, and he lit up her blood by simply breathing. She wanted him to tell her more, to explain why his brother was rolling around in jewels while he was digging out muck. She wanted to uncover all of his secrets until she understood what made him tick and how to get him to kiss her again.

Damn it.

She wasn't supposed to want that. Asher wasn't hers. She wasn't his. They were putting this on for show, and she'd be going home in a few weeks. Inconvenient feelings for a busy dragon lord couldn't be part of the plan.

The path led to a small gazebo with a roof latticed with those dark vines. It let moonlight peek in.

"I think this is my favorite part of the planet," Asher said. "We only finished it about a month ago. There were so many other priorities to sort out first. I had to help the grounds staff before the blooms started to wither. If we'd lost them, I don't know that Lady Nova would have approved another shipment. I already had to fight to get the first shipment approved."

"I'm glad I'm here to see it." This was the first time Asher seemed passionate about something on this place. Sure, he gave every ounce of his attention to his duties, but he hadn't smiled. Ever since they'd walked through the door, his mouth had quirked up and he seemed younger, freer.

Happy.

Maybe her dragon man needed a garden, not a planet.

Not hers.

His brow furrowed. "Is something wrong?" He leaned in closer as he asked.

It was the perfect romantic moment. A gazebo

made of nocturnal flowers, an unfamiliar moon overhead, and the most gorgeous man she'd ever seen looking at her like she mattered.

Zoe wanted to kiss him so much that it hurt. She had to choke back her thought about his gardening aptitude. It wasn't her place to say anything like that, and she refused to ruin this moment.

This thing between them could never be real, but in the dark she was happy to play pretend.

Asher breathed deep and his dark eyes took on a strange, orangish hue, almost as if embers burned deep inside of them. He raised his hand and traced his fingers over her cheekbone.

Zoe's tongue darted out to lick her lips. If he leaned in an inch, she was jumping him, no question. Her body sang with need, and at the moment she didn't care that it was temporary. If she could only have him for a night, she'd take it.

But Asher dropped his hand and looked away.

She tried not to feel disappointed.

"You probably have to get back to work," she said, scrambling for an excuse. "Or maybe you'll actually sleep?" She saw the dark circles under his eyes and hoped they were temporary. This man needed a nap like nobody's business.

He shook his head. "There's always more to do. I'll head to sleep in a few hours. Before dawn, I promise."

"The sooner you get back, the sooner you can sleep, I guess." Keeping her tone light was an effort. She wanted to insist he go back to his room and sleep for a day. It would probably only make him stay up even later.

"Are you doing anything tomorrow?" he asked.

She shook her head. "My schedule is open." It was hard to be busy when there wasn't anything for her to do except walk through the gardens.

"There's some place I'd like to show you. Will you go with me?" The hope in his voice had her heartrate kicking up.

Oh, this was bad. So, so bad. Neither of them was supposed to be getting their hopes up. They weren't supposed to want anything.

Too late.

"I'll go," she agreed.

Asher's smile bloomed just as broadly as the flowers around them, and Zoe couldn't help but smile back.

Screw *supposed to*. Wherever this dragon was taking her, she was ready for the ride.

CHAPTER NINE

By early afternoon, Zoe was beginning to think Asher was standing her up. She'd sprung out of bed the moment she opened her eyes, eager for whatever adventure her mysterious dragon was determined to bring her on.

He hadn't been waiting for her in the dining hall, but she didn't let that disappoint her. He was a busy man, and if he was taking hours out of his day, then surely he had some stuff to tie up before they took off.

But as the hours of morning ticked by and turned to afternoon without even a note, Zoe had to wonder if last night's promises and hopes had been conjured by the spell of the night garden. Asher must have come to his senses and remembered that he didn't have to waste any time on her and this fake thing between them.

So she did the only thing she could ever think to do now: went for a walk in the Verdant Sector. Everyone else was too busy to talk to her, but the flowers and plants didn't care.

Homesickness rocked her as she walked by a cluster of plants that looked like miniature sunflowers, her mother's favorite bloom.

Zoe blinked several times, refusing to let a single tear fall. She'd buried her mother and left the grief behind. She had to if she was going to carve a life for herself.

But what would that life even mean once she got back? Assuming it hadn't been blown up all to hell with her disappearance.

Her fascination with space began and ended with the question of alien life. And now? Question answered. Unequivocally. Aliens were out there and they were sexy.

What was she going to do about it, though? She couldn't just make a declaration and call it good. Her peers wanted research, data, *proof*. Her story might get her a feature documentary on one of the zanier streaming services, but she'd never prove it to anyone that mattered.

Why did she care?

Zoe had been miserable for the past several months, every bit of research feeling like another piece of an impossible to solve puzzle that would drive her mad before she made any progress.

She could just walk away.

The thought stole her breath. She'd worked so hard for all of these years. She was determined to become Zoe Gershwin, PhD and live up to all of her mother's dreams for her.

But her mom would have wanted her to be happy more than anything.

What made her happy?

"Am I interrupting you?" Asher asked, startling her enough to make her jump in place.

Zoe clamped a hand over her chest, eyes wide. "Crap, you scared me." Her heart thundered but was quickly calming down.

"My apologies. I'd hoped to find you earlier, but there were more preparations than I anticipated. There was a small fire in the eastern thresher repository last night."

"Was anyone hurt?" She took a closer look at Asher and noticed the dark smudges under his eyes were even darker than usual. "Did you sleep? Do you have to cancel?"

He smiled and took her hand, leading her down the path back towards the compound. "No one was injured, the repository is completely automated, and the fire suppression system did eventually kick in. I managed a bit of sleep, and there is very little that would make me cancel this outing. Are you ready to go?" He squeezed her hand. "Everything is prepared for us, so there's no need to pack."

"Pack? What do you have in store? Where are we going?" The terror of that first day, of the machine bearing down on her and the unbelievable rescue by Asher, still snared her in nightmares. But no matter what, she couldn't be scared of Asher's monstrous form.

Everything about him was gorgeous to her.

His smile grew broader. "Don't you like surprises?"

"The last surprise I had landed me on an alien planet." But she didn't pull away.

He stepped in close, so close that narrowing the distance between them would be effortless. Flames seemed to dance in his eyes, and the desire to kiss him was so strong that Zoe could feel a fire of her own smoldering deep inside of her.

Why did the perfect guy need to be a workaholic dragon from another planet?

"Just trust me, Zoe," he said.

She nodded, not quite able to find the words.

He led her to the edge of the Verdant Sector, into a giant dirt area with no cultivated plants, though a few valiant weeds were making the effort. "Stand back," he warned. "I'm going to shift."

"Are you... am I—how are we travelling to this mysterious place?"

His grin made her stomach flip. Oh, she had it bad and there was no escaping it.

When she was about twenty feet back, Asher took a deep breath. And then he was a dragon. There was no painful rending of clothes and skin, no massive swirl of dust and glitter and light. He was just *there* and a dragon.

Her mouth dropped open in amazement and she had to quash the urge to laugh. "You look freaking amazing."

Thank you. His voice rang in her head, and she couldn't tell whether or not she was imagining it.

Zoe had already taken things too far and she couldn't deal with any more craziness, so she ignored the possible telepathy. She'd ask him when he looked human again.

Asher flattened himself to the ground and she realized she was supposed to climb on his back. He was bigger than a semi-truck and probably would be less stable once they got into the air. But she knew he wouldn't let her fall, not if there was anything he could do to stop it.

She clambered up onto his back and found a hand-hold where some of his skin bunched. Apparently dragons didn't come with seatbelts, so she flattened herself against his back and clenched her legs around a hump in his spine.

Then they were off.

Every muscle in Zoe's body tensed for the first minutes of the flight, certain she would fall off. But as the beat of Asher's wings evened out and they soared through the air, she got her bearings and started to feel a bit more confident. She didn't fully let go, but she loosened her grip enough so that she didn't hurt herself.

"How many people have you flown like this?" she yelled into the wind, not expecting an answer.

I've never dropped anyone. The words rang in her head.

Zoe laughed. "That's not an answer!"

Asher seemed to jolt under her, and they dropped a few feet before he evened out again.

Zoe patted a hand against his scales. "Everything alright?" But there was no reply.

They flew low over the land, and its stark beauty

caught her breath. Most of it was barren, with only a few ponds of water and struggling greenery breaking up the sand and rock. Then they passed over a section that had been treated by the terraformers, and it was a different world: grassy and growing as if they'd just flown over a prairie.

The next patch of untreated land was crawling with the same lizard-kitties she'd seen at the compound, hundreds of them that all ran for cover when Asher's shadow passed overhead.

Then there was more greenery, but this didn't look anything like the terraformed prairieland, it appeared to be a small patch of jungle that looked like it had been growing undisturbed for millennia. Except for the small cottage hidden among the vines right at the edge between jungle and desert.

Asher landed gently and Zoe disembarked and backed far enough away to allow him to shift forms. Once he was human again, he stared at her, eyes dancing with flames, but she couldn't read his expression. Then it cleared, and he nodded towards the cottage.

"Our castle, Miss Gershwin." He held out a hand.

She stepped closer and placed her hand in his, the weight of it warm and inviting. She had it bad for this dragon.

Of course no normal human guy would ever do it for her, she'd been waiting to meet this one.

Two lizard-kitties crossed their path as they walked up to the cottage. "There are so many of them here," she said, resisting the urge to kneel down and summon one.

"The threshers destroy their dens, which is why there aren't too many near the compound. By the time this planet is terraformed, there won't be many left."

"That's terrible." Now she wanted to chase after the animal and find a place it might be safe. "Isn't there something you can do?"

Asher had the decency to look a little ashamed. "Not really, I'm afraid. Come on inside."

Zoe stared at the streak in the sand where the lizard-kitties had scampered off to before looking away. All progress had a cost, but was it worth it?

The worries fell to the back of her mind once they were through the door. The place was like a fairytale cottage. Dark wood beams stretched from one end of the ceiling to the other, with whitewashed walls decorated with lush paintings of landscapes she didn't recognize.

Intricately carved wooden furniture filled the room, and a huge hearth took up one wall, the fire blazing to life with one burst of flame from Asher's hands.

"What is this place?" she asked. It was so different from the compound and its sterile utility.

He ran his fingers over the edge of the sofa, and Zoe tried not to imagine what those fingers would feel like on her skin. "It's my sanctuary. I slowly built it during my leave time. I needed a place I could escape."

"You *built* this place? With your own hands?" She took it in again in amazement. She felt accomplished when she finished a small Lego set. He'd built an entire freaking house like he was Paul Bunyan or something.

"My hands and the help of some builder-bots. Do you like it?" He was vulnerable in a way she'd never seen from him as he asked it.

Zoe nodded, words still a bit hard to find.

"Let me give you the tour."

The simplicity of the house made sense now that she knew he'd built it. It was mostly one large room with a bed off in one corner and a small kitchen in the other, and the living room dominated by that hearth and furniture. The perfect little hideaway for a busy dragon.

And he'd shared it with her.

Her heartbeat kicked up. This wasn't some simple

little thing to share with his temporary and fake human fiancée. This was a special place.

"Do you bring people here often?" she forced herself to ask, even as she was almost certain of the answer.

"Remy's been here a couple of times."

"Just your sister?"

He nodded. "I don't want... that is... this is my special place. I don't want to share it."

"You shared it with me."

"I did." He swallowed, his throat bobbing.

"Why?" Her tongue darted out to wet her lips, her hands trembled with the need to touch him. This wasn't some simple gesture.

This was everything.

She had to look away, just for a second, before she said something that would give too much away. But her gaze fell on the bed just behind him, and her breath caught in her throat.

Asher stilled. This was his place, he didn't need to turn around to know what was where. But after a breath, he slowly turned his head and took in the bed. Then he turned back to her.

There was another breath, there must have been. And then his mouth was on hers. His hands found their way to the small of her back, drawing her closer to him so there was no space between them.

His own heart was a beating drum thudding against her chest, and hers returned the rhythm. Zoe wrapped her arms around his neck and surrendered to it, needing only this moment.

His fingers teased under her shirt, and goose-bumps exploded everywhere he touched. She would have ripped her shirt off if it didn't mean breaking the kiss, but she wasn't willing to put a single breath between her lips and his.

If kissing him in the Verdant Sector had rocked her to the core, this thing now remade her, burned her to a crisp, blew away the ashes, and reforged her into a creature made of heat and want.

Want for Asher.

Need.

It was a primal, possessive sort of yearning, some-thing she'd never felt before but knew she couldn't give up. He was under her skin, in her blood, in her very soul. She didn't know how she was supposed to walk away from him.

And from the way his fingers clenched on her hips, he was feeling the same.

His lips trailed down her throat, a hint of teeth nipping at her skin. Her back arched as she gasped for air. She wanted more from him, and the need threatened to overwhelm her.

His fingers brushed against her skin until his palm was flat against her back, hot enough to brand her, to mark her forever. She could already feel the shift in herself, the way this kiss was changing her, as if a space inside of her heart was opening for Asher—and only for Asher.

Forever.

It should have terrified her, but passion overwhelmed any sort of fear.

She could feel the press of his cock, hot and hard between them, and she moaned, the sound primitive in its need. All she could feel now was desire, it was her only want. Desire for Asher, for what he could do to her, with her.

Between one moment and the next, her shirt disappeared, yanked over her head before she realized he was trying to remove it. The built-in bra went with it, leaving her naked from the waist up under the fire of Asher's gaze.

Her nipples tightened, her body wet and eager for more.

Slowly, she reached out and slid her hand between the buttons of his shirt, snapping them open, one by one, until she revealed Asher's naked skin. She pushed the shirt off his shoulders and flattened her palms against the hard planes of his chest.

Unable to stop herself, she leaned in close and kissed his nipple, smiling against his skin as he groaned.

He buried his fingers in her hair and pulled her back, and when she saw his eyes, they were completely inhuman, consumed by the flames that marked him as a dragon. This close to him, she could see the faint outline of some mark on his skin, almost like the subtlest tattoo. But, no, this was something he'd been born with, the dim mark of the scales he wore in his other form.

He kissed her, his lips trailing along her jaw, his teeth nibbling on her ear, and her mind whirled, his touch consuming her. "I didn't bring you here for this," he whispered, his voice dark.

Her fingers clenched, refusing to let him pull back. "Do you want to stop?" If he said yes, she had to let him go, had to find a way to be okay with that.

He shuddered, his breath a whisper over her throat. "No, I don't."

"Good." She captured his mouth and kissed him again.

It was all the permission he needed, and his hands tightened in her hair, holding her still as he explored her with his mouth. He trailed down her throat and across her collarbone, his lips hot and hungry.

The rough scrape of his stubble tickled her skin as he nuzzled against her. Then his palms were on her skin, moving over her body. Her mind whirled as the desire, the ache between her legs intensified. She needed more, and when he closed his lips over one of her nipples, the moan that ripped out of her throat echoed around the room.

He suckled, his tongue swirling, teasing, and she gripped his shoulders, her head falling back. When he nipped at her, she cried out. His teeth scraped against her tender skin, the pain sharp and glorious. He moved his mouth, shifting so that he could capture the other nipple, his fingers stroking over her stomach and her thighs, barely touching her, and she bucked, desperate for him.

"Please, Asher, more." It was needy, vulnerable, and she would promise him anything if only he would promise to keep touching her forever. They were in their own little world here, far away from anyone else, and tonight she could pretend that she really was his. Nothing in this room was fake.

His breath was harsh as he pulled back to watch her. His gaze was wild, a dark hunger reflected back at her, and she shivered at the sheer intensity. He hefted her up and took the two final steps to the bed, laying her down with a gentleness that belied the intensity of his expression.

He stood, his hands still resting on her thighs, his thumbs stroking her skin. Her heart beat frantically, and she licked her lips, staring up at him. She was spread out before him like a feast, and he was going to devour her.

He leaned over her, hand moving slowly until it hovered over the clasp of her pants. Zoe was frozen in place, prey under this predator's gaze. And when his fingers undid her pants, she watched as he pulled them off, breath heaving out of him until she was completely naked and waiting.

Before she could lean in to strip him, he pushed off his pants and stood before her, cock hard and proud and all for her. The sight of him sent a shiver racing down her spine. She needed this.

Zoe grabbed his wrist and yanked him down on top of her, wrapping her arms around him as she kissed him. He moaned, and the sound was so damn sexy that she couldn't help but run her hand down his stomach and wrap her fingers around his erection.

He grunted, his body bucking as she squeezed her fingers. She wanted to do things to him, to see him fall apart as he lost himself in her, and the thought made her ache. She stroked him, wanting him to feel the same desire that had her panting.

"I need you, please." If she waited any longer, she might expire from her smoldering need.

His breath was a stuttered gasp as he pushed her legs open. He stroked his finger over her, and she writhed, trying to get him to touch her properly. But he leaned forward and caught her earlobe between his teeth, making her shudder.

"Please, Asher." She needed him.

He growled, his lips traveling down her throat. He sucked, and she cried out.

His finger stroked over her once more, and she dug her fingers into his back, trying to keep herself grounded as the pleasure threatened to consume her. She wanted him inside her, filling her up, and the feeling was almost unbearable. She reached down, her fingers closing around him, and his eyes flew open, burning with heat. He was as desperate for her as she was for him, and the knowledge made her body tremble.

His cock teased her entrance, and then he was pushing inside of her. She moaned, her back arching. God, he was big, bigger than she expected, and it had been some time since she'd last had a lover. But she reveled in the feeling of him stretching her, and he watched her face, his gaze intent. He slid deeper, and the discomfort gave way to the pure bliss of feeling him inside.

He pulled back, leaving her empty, and then thrust forward, burying himself completely inside of her. He cursed, his eyes flaring with fire as his jaw clenched and he held himself back. She wanted him to let go, to unleash his fury of desire on her, and she clenched her muscles, trying to hold him in place and reveling in the sound of his groan.

She could get used to this.

But Asher wasn't done with her. He withdrew, and then thrust inside again, harder this time, and a cry burst from her. Her fingers gripped his skin, trying to hold onto something. She was going to fall, and if he let go, she would have nothing to stop her.

Her body arched, meeting his thrusts. The pleasure built, and when she felt herself cresting, she fell. Her mind blanked, and the only thing left was the pleasure. It consumed her, and she went limp as he came with a draconic roar.

She came back to herself with Asher hovering over her. He was trembling, his whole body taut. But his eyes were dark, his gaze fixed on her.

He lowered his head, his lips brushing against hers. "I didn't know I needed this. You."

She tried to find the words to say something back, but her heart was too busy falling just as hard as her body just had, her emotions so tangled up in the dragon beside her that she feared she might never recover.

CHAPTER TEN

ASHER COULDN'T TAKE his eyes off Zoe. His body still hummed from the pleasure of their night together and he wanted to stay in this cottage for the rest of the week. Or possibly forever. It didn't matter that Remy was expecting him back today and that, no doubt, work had piled up on his desk. He wanted to soak up more time with his...

With Zoe. She could be nothing more to him than Zoe, even if a suspicion was beginning to nag deep in his mind.

She'd spoken to him on the flight here, had heard his voice in her mind. A normal human shouldn't have been able to. But his mate could. Was Zoe...?

He shoved the thought aside. He didn't have time for a mate, certainly not now. And he'd make a terrible one anyway, too obsessed with his work to be the kind of partner a woman like Zoe deserved.

What was he thinking? Asher didn't need or want a mate. He couldn't stand to be in the company of most people for more than a matter of hours, and people could stand him for even less time. He was an exacting and annoying boss, and too ambitious for someone who wanted the freedom to discover everything the universe had to show.

So why did he want to offer to run away with her and show her that universe?

"We have to go," he forced out. They were finishing the last of the small breakfast he'd prepared for them. He'd been taking tiny bites, hoping to prolong the final minutes.

Zoe frowned for a moment and then shrugged and forced a smile. "Thanks for bringing me here. This has been..." She swallowed and then blushed.

A grin bloomed on his own face as he remembered the way she'd moaned beneath him. Truly, he hadn't brought her here for sex, but he'd hold these memories close for the rest of his life.

Could he convince her to stay?

"Is something wrong?" Zoe asked. She leaned forward and placed her hand over his.

"Why?" He didn't pull away. Once they returned to

reality he'd have to behave, have to remember that nothing between them could last longer than this month. Lady Nova would see that Zoe wasn't an appropriate wife for the Lord-Governor of VMC12 and that would be that.

"You started frowning just then." She gave his hand a squeeze and then let go.

Even if he knew what to say to get her to stay on VMC12 with him, he'd be a monster for trying it. She deserved the entire universe, not the tiny corner of a planet with its drab gray walls and constant work. If he wanted to keep her, he needed to give her everything.

He couldn't.

He didn't need a wife. He didn't deserve a mate, and he couldn't keep Zoe.

"Are you ready to go?" he asked, forcing himself to stand. "I'll wait for you in the front of the house." He didn't wait for her to respond.

Asher transformed to his other form while waiting for Zoe. He had a feeling she might want to talk, and he couldn't risk that, as he didn't know what he'd say. In his dragon form he let his muscles stretch out, arching his behind into the air and flaring out his wings to their broadest span. He longed for the feel of the wind beneath him, but with Zoe on his back, he'd have to fly with care. He would let no harm come to her.

His ears twitched when he heard the door to the cottage open and close, and then Zoe's scent engulfed him. A sound of pleasure rumbled in his chest.

"Are you purring?" she asked, placing a hand on his sensitive flank as she clambered up onto his back.

He kept his thoughts to himself this time. She couldn't be his mate, but if she could understand him through some strange quirk, he wasn't going to give anything away.

He launched himself into the air, climbing carefully and at a much shallower pitch than he preferred. It took much more energy to fly so low, the wind buffeting him from all ends. If he flew higher, he could ride the currents and let the planet's wind do most of the work for him, gliding freely over most of the distance. But that would be too cold for the human on his back, the air too thin. He wouldn't take the risk.

They flew for hours, covering a distance that would have taken more than a day to walk, but were only a little more than halfway to their destination. That was when smoke tickled his nose.

Asher wanted to ignore it, but he had a duty to investigate. If something was wrong, he could send out a crew once they got home. But he needed to know what he was sending that crew out for.

He followed the scent and found the plume after another minute, a dark cloud of black smoke billowing into the air and emanating from one of the terraforming threshers that was making an awful grinding sound.

Damnation. VMC12 was eating up threshers like it had a taste for them. This was the fourth thresher in a year and if they couldn't repair it, it would be months before they received a new one. But there was nothing he could do now.

He circled the machine to see if he could identify a source of the damage, but he couldn't see anything that he could report to the recovery team.

The thresher screeched, and Asher pumped his wings. He didn't like that sound, and with Zoe on his back, he needed to get away in case the thresher failed catastrophically.

That was the idea, at least. But the thresher exploded with a bang, and he'd only begun to realize it happened when searing pain tore through his wing and he began to plummet towards the ground.

Zoe's scream rang in his ears, and he forced his mangled wing to stretch, hoping to manage as much of a glide as he could.

He crashed to the ground at a speed high enough to hurt his bones, but Zoe was still clutching the ruff on his back, and hadn't been flung off. That was good. For now. His wing screamed in pain and he had to be losing blood. They were too far from anywhere to call for help, and the burning metal of the thresher was close enough to be the real threat.

Zoe scampered off his back and Asher forced himself to shift, screaming in pain as his voice came back to him. The shift wouldn't fix his wing, but it stopped any bleeding. For now. He could feel the deep gouge of an injury on his back and knew that moving forward at all would be excruciating.

The winds around them were wild. Zoe's hair whipped around her head, and she kept trying to tuck it behind her ears, but it wouldn't stay put. Asher staggered over to her, acrid smoke burning its way into his lungs. He was a dragon—breathing smoke was as easy as breathing air—so if this was bothering him, it had to be monstrous for his human.

She coughed and then pulled up her shirt to cover her mouth. "Are you okay?" she yelled over the roaring wind.

He didn't have an answer for that. His shirt felt wet and he hoped it was sweat from the heat, but didn't dare try to find out. "Come on!" He put an arm around her and tugged her away from the smoldering heap of the thresher. He had to get her clear. He could smother the flames with his own fire, but not with Zoe so close.

She went with him, limping a little but otherwise unharmed.

Asher set her down on a boulder beyond the worst of the rubble and turned back towards the disaster.

"Your back!" Zoe yelled. Fingers touched his shoulder as she tried to stop him.

"Later! I need to do this." He pulled away and strode towards the fire, trusting she was smart enough to stay put.

The wind was a monster of its own, stoking the fire whenever it might have died on its own. It was an inferno by the time he made his way back to the heart of it. Asher summoned his own flame, the ember inside of him burning low from all the energy he'd expelled in the flight, but that didn't matter now. A dragon's flame was stronger than any natural fire, and once he took control of the fire here, all would be well.

But it was harder than it should have been, and he had to stretch and stretch his flame, covering more of the wreckage and reaching dangerously close to Zoe. He didn't pull back, even as the edge of his flame battled with a smoldering holdout so close to his human that he knew she could feel the heat.

Something pressed against his flame, and it wasn't the thresher's own fire. He glanced at Zoe and saw her hands in front of her as if she was warding off the fire herself. But she flinched away, and the pressure abated.

Impossible.

He couldn't think of it now, not when the thresher's fire still smoldered. It took several more minutes, but he managed to smother it all and staggered back towards Zoe, collapsing, exhausted, on the boulder beside her. He leaned his head against her shoulder, needing the comfort of her touch as the reality of their situation crashed over him.

They were a day's walk from anywhere, and he didn't think he could stand up again.

CHAPTER ELEVEN

Something was wrong with Zoe's hands. And something was even more wrong with Asher. His shoulder slumped, back curved in a half-circle, and his chest heaved with every breath. His shirt was soaked through with something darker than sweat and they didn't have any bandages.

She could ignore the strange way her fingers tingled and the nagging sensation that she'd done something to affect Asher's fire. She couldn't ignore his injuries.

The air around them was acrid with smoke, but she didn't see any fire from the scattered parts of the machine. They didn't have a map, she didn't have a phone, and she wasn't sure if Asher had some way to contact the compound.

Exactly how far away from civilization—such as it was—were they?

Zoe reached out, but left her arm hovering over Asher's shoulder, unsure of whether touching him might make everything worse.

In the distance she spotted a patch of green with a single tree valiantly climbing out of the sand. If there was greenery, there might be water, and it would be better than laying down to die amid the wreckage of the thresher.

She just hoped that Asher could walk.

"We're going to go there." She pointed to their destination and then repeated the instruction when Asher looked at her blankly. "There," she repeated, and jabbed her finger towards the tree. "Would there be anything in the wreckage we can use? Fabric? Blankets?" As far as she knew, no person was supposed to touch the machines, but she didn't know all of their secrets.

Asher shook his head, dashing her hopes that there might be a first aid kit. Oh well. No time to worry now.

"Can you stand?" she asked. She wanted to get herself under his arm and prop him up, but wanted him to try and move under his own power first.

He took several deep breaths before planting his

hands on his legs and heaving himself up with a pained groan. He took two staggering steps in the right direction before he stumbled, and then Zoe was there, wedging herself under his arm and leading the way.

The man was heavy, and injured enough that he'd given her a good chunk of his weight. She wasn't about to complain, not now, not when she heard the gasping pain of every third step.

Walking through the sand weighed her down just as much as half-carrying Asher did, and the oasis seemed to remain the same distance away, no matter how far they walked. After several minutes, she began to worry that it was some kind of mirage, a trick in the desert that would lead to both of them frying under the unforgiving heat of the sun.

But then they crested a small dune and began downhill, and suddenly the oasis was both closer and bigger than it had appeared in the distance. Zoe let out a sob of relief and picked up her pace until Asher began groaning with every step.

He needed a doctor, or at least someplace clean. The most medical training she had came from a half-forgotten merit badge for first aid from her one year in Girl Scouts, so she wouldn't be much help.

They entered the oasis and the broad leaves of the

tree cast shade over a spot covered in soft moss. It looked like heaven, and Zoe carefully laid Asher down, trying to avoid making him lean on his injured flank.

He blinked his eyes open and stared at her as she took the place in. His gaze was steady, not the haze of pain and fever she worried she might see.

A small pond filled with plants that looked a bit like lily pads was encircled by tall grass. The water was murky, but she spotted a few fish swimming and a bird sitting on one of the pads. That probably meant it was clean enough... right?

Maybe she should have done more than a year of Girl Scouts, though she didn't think there was a merit badge for identifying alien life.

"Give me your shirt." She held out a hand.

"What?" His voice was pained but clear.

"I'm going to dump it in the water and then try and clean your back. How bad is it?" Before this was over, she might end up using her own shirt as a bandage, but maybe they'd get a lucky break.

She was pretty sure that lucky break had been used up in surviving the explosion.

"It hurts," Asher said as he pulled the shirt over his head. He laid down on his stomach, and she got a good look at the nasty bruise circling a wound which oozed a trickle of thick blood.

She winced, but was relieved. The flow of blood didn't look too bad, even if it had to hurt like hell. Zoe took his shirt and carefully rinsed it in the pond until it was clean of dirt and blood and sand. She wrung it out as best as she could and then slowly walked back over to the resting dragon.

"This is probably going to hurt even more," she warned. "But we don't want it getting infected. Can dragons even get infections?" Either way, she wanted his wound clean.

He hissed as she pressed the makeshift rag against his back. "We can," he gritted out. "But this should heal quickly." He hissed again as she scraped over a particularly sensitive spot.

Zoe didn't let his distress stop her. A bit of pain now would make things better later. It *would* be worth it. It had to be.

"Okay, I think that's enough. Stay on your stomach." She couldn't have him rolling over and ruining all her hard work.

She dunked the shirt in the water again and then wrung it out again before hanging it on the lowest branch of the tree to dry. Finally satisfied, she sat down beside Asher, her back to the tree.

He made a displeased sound and she surged forward.

"What's wrong?" Had she missed something? Was he bleeding internally?

"I can't see you," he said, sounding a bit put out by that.

She let out a relieved laugh and changed her position so she was laying down beside him. Their heads were only a few inches apart, but there was no chance of anything happening now, not with him so injured and there being so much sand around them.

"What do we do now?" she asked. She hadn't been able to think beyond getting them to the oasis and cleaning Asher's wound. Her brain was fried, and she was happy to lay here until they were magically rescued.

"Communicator." He shifted his position, trying to reach into his pocket.

"Let me," she said, reaching for him. But she found both of his pockets empty. "Could it be anywhere else?"

"Fell out." His words were barely more than grunts.

She was afraid of that. "Any other ideas?"

He reached out and clasped their hands together, entwining their fingers. "Someone will come to investigate the thresher. Tomorrow morning at the latest. They'll find us." He didn't sound too worried.

Zoe decided to believe it was true. This was Asher's planet, he knew the protocols. If he said someone was coming, they'd come. "I don't suppose we can hike back to the cottage?" She wasn't eager to get up, but there was food and a bed back there.

He shook his head. "We're more than halfway to the compound. It's a day's walk either way."

"You fly fast." It had been exhilarating up in the air with him, but she hadn't realized just how fast they were going. "Do you ever race?"

"Only every time I see my brothers." There was a smile in his voice.

"Do you win?" She asked both to keep him talking and because she was desperate to soak up any bit of knowledge she could learn about this man.

"When Flint and Knox don't cheat."

She laughed. "It sounds nice."

"What?" He squeezed her hand and their gazes locked.

Zoe's heart flipped over. She had it so bad for this guy and was steaming straight ahead into heartbreak.

What would he do if she kissed him right now?

She forced herself to talk instead. "Having a big family. It was always just me and my mom back home. Until... well, now it's just me."

He squeezed her hand again. "I'm sorry about

that. My parents would be crazy about you."

"Really? They wouldn't care that I'm human?" He made it sound like such a dealbreaker for his boss. And wasn't he a lord? Shouldn't *he* care about that?

"If I'm happy, they're happy. And they've wanted me to be happy for a very long time."

"Are you?" He invited the question, but asking felt beyond intrusive. Still, she couldn't help herself.

"Never happier." The confession hung between them.

She had to say something, to give him something back to make him understand that she knew exactly what he meant, even if it was impossible. There was no place she'd rather be than laying beside him, even if they were both dirty and hurt and reeling from nearly being exploded.

"I think I did something to your fire," she said, wincing at her own subject change. "How is that possible? It was like I waved my hand and it did what I wanted." She needed the explanation, needed some way to make sense of the impossible.

But after more than a minute, Asher didn't answer. His eyes had drifted closed and his breath evened out.

The injured dragon was asleep.

Zoe's answers would have to wait.

CHAPTER TWELVE

ASHER'S entire body ached as the rescue transport landed in the airfield outside the compound. As predicted, a crew had come to check on the destroyed thresher and discovered him and Zoe.

He didn't relish a night spent on hot sand, but a part of him was disappointed to be back. He knew there would be a mountain of thankless work waiting for him, and he'd no doubt be swallowed up. Zoe would go back to exploring the compound without him, and before he knew it, she'd be gone.

Unless he did something about that.

But he didn't know what he *could* do, short of making a declaration and begging her to stay.

The thought was more tempting by the minute.

Cirk met them the moment they stepped into the

compound, two gurneys ready to be floated down to the med bay to tend to any wounds.

"Climb on," Asher told Zoe, reaching for her arm to assist her.

She gave him a doubtful look. "You're the one that's hurt. I'm fine, just a bit thirsty." She turned to the doctor. "You have to look at his back. His wing got injured in our flight and he's bruised to high heaven. He keeps wincing."

"I'm fine," Asher insisted through gritted teeth. "It hurts a lot less today."

Cirk's gaze bounced between them, lips pursed. "Great, now there's two of you. You're both getting checked out. You can walk to med bay or you can get on the gurneys, but if either of you collapse, I'm keeping you all day."

Zoe took another look at the gurney, but shook her head. "I can walk."

Asher was going to make it on his own two feet if it killed him.

He took Zoe's hand as they marched through the halls, just a step behind Cirk. He didn't care if anyone saw or commented. No, he was happy if they did. He'd claimed this woman and wanted to proclaim it to the entire kingdom.

Had she really controlled his flame? Could she

really be his mate?

The possibilities swirled as he walked, making the pain easier to ignore. It had dulled, but it wouldn't fully recede until the underlying injury was healed.

Once they were in the infirmary, Cirk scanned them both and declared them well enough to go. Asher had instructions to shift into his other form for no less than two hours a day for two weeks, but to not fly for more than fifteen minutes until all the pain was gone. Then the doctor left them alone.

"I have to get back to work," he said with some reluctance.

Zoe cradled his head in her hands and leaned in to kiss him. It was gentle at first, but he swept his tongue in and she moaned beneath him, her hands sliding down to clutch at his shoulders.

His blood roared with need and he wanted to sweep her off her feet and lay her down on the nearest flat surface—probably an examination table—and have his way with her.

Instead he forced himself to pull back. They were back in the real world and he had a duty.

"Have dinner with me in my private quarters tonight?" he asked, already planning out the meal. He didn't care about putting on a show for others, he wanted to spend time with his human. "And stay the night?"

She grinned. "I'll see if I can clear my busy schedule." She kissed his cheek and backed out of his embrace. "I'm going to go take an hour long shower. At least clean yourself before you dive behind your desk?"

"As you command, my lady." The need to kiss her was too strong to resist, but he made it quick before he forced himself to walk away.

He took the shower, but had to make it quick. The morning was already gone, wasted in rescue and transport. He'd only cleared his schedule for a single day, but was now well into the second day gone. Remy had to be ready to kill him, and he wouldn't be surprised if something other than the thresher had exploded.

He found his sister in his office, her clothing rumpled as if she'd slept there. There were dark bags under her eyes and she glared at him as he entered.

"I'm sorry I lost contact," he said and braced himself for her verbal fire.

"*That's* why you're sorry? I thought you were dead!" She launched herself out of the seat and wrapped him up in a tight hug. "I couldn't get you on comms and then you didn't show up. I was two minutes away from sending in the troops when the team found that downed thresher and then the two of you. Are you okay?"

Somehow in the course of the hug they'd switched positions. Asher took his own seat while Remy sat on the opposite side of his desk. "I'm fine," he replied. "Cirk gave Zoe and I the okay. Just a bit banged up. I'll be all healed before you know it."

A strange look crossed his sister's face, but it was gone in a blink and Asher wondered if he'd really seen it. "How are you not dead?" she demanded.

"I am a dragon," he reminded her.

"Not that! You could take down a legion. I've been doing your job for one day and I don't know how you haven't collapsed in exhaustion. It's the work of six people. I started delegating what I could. You really need to learn to trust people more. And you know that irrigation issue in Sector Three? Wrede sent you a message on how to fix it more than a month ago! I gave him the go ahead and things should be fixed by the end of the day today."

"It's fixed?" The irrigation issue in Sector Three had been a thorn in his side for awhile now, but Wrede's messages were always too long by half and filled with sorry excuses and bad jokes. Asher had started skimming them after awhile and ignoring the worst of them. Apparently that was a mistake.

"All good," Remy confirmed. "Do you really..." She trailed off.

"Do I really what?"

"Never mind." She stood up and came around the desk. "Let me show you what I did."

"I was only gone for a day!" He feared he'd have a lot to fix, but now it appeared that Remy had upset his entire system.

Maybe she should be the one in charge.

"There's also this." She shuffled through a mysterious pile of folders on the desk and handed him one with a frustratingly familiar seal.

"I don't need the Agency, I have a fiancée," he reminded her. A *fake* fiancée, technically. Whatever she was, Asher was done with the Intergalactic Dating Agency. "I think she might be my mate," he admitted out loud for the first time.

"I know." Remy shoved the folder at him again.

He snatched it out of her hand before she could smack him with it. "How can you know? I don't even know!" It was only a feeling and a bit of evidence. He needed to explore things further and see what Zoe felt about the whole thing. Remy couldn't know anything.

"Read the file."

Asher flipped it open and skimmed. Then he spotted the picture of Zoe and he scowled.

What?

Why?

How?

Zoe hadn't said a word about the IDA. They'd spoken about it, he remembered. He'd told her about his search to find a bride. He'd specifically mentioned the agency. And she hadn't said a word.

But the file right here had her listed as a client who'd signed up for their services more than a month ago. And it had somehow identified *him* as her mate.

How could they know that?

Rumor had it that the IDA employed psychics to aid in the matching process, but that was just marketing. They couldn't really know.

Why had Zoe lied?

"She consented to be transported to you," Remy said, pointing out a line low down on the page. "This is her signature."

Right there in black ink, he saw it.

He slammed the file shut and glared at his sister. He couldn't think of what to say.

"What do you want to do about it?" she asked. "You should probably talk to her. Find out her side of the story."

"Her side of the story is pretty clear. We both knew that nonsense about the game was beyond belief. I can't believe I..." He smelled smoke and looked down to see the paper of the file blackening around his fingers. He lifted up his hand and glared at his smoking skin. If he saw Zoe right now, there was no telling what he'd say. And even with this betrayal, he refused to risk hurting her.

"Get her out of here," he said. "Send her home. It's done."

CHAPTER THIRTEEN

Zoe kept smiling like she was a kid with a secret. It had to look weird because she'd received more than one strange look. She couldn't bring herself to care. Her body was still buzzing from the two nights with Asher, even if one had not exactly been the pleasurable fantasy she might have wished for.

She wanted time with him. And she was going to get it.

She'd fallen completely and she just had to live with it. Yes, she was barreling straight towards heartbreak, but that was a couple of weeks away. She was going to soak up every feeling, every memory she could, so when she was forlornly staring at her equations back home with nothing but cold stars and math to keep her company, at least she would know that she'd once loved a dragon.

What would Asher say if she told him she didn't want to leave? Well, at least, she didn't want to leave *him.* VMC12 was kind of boring and she'd need to find something to do, but that didn't mean she had to leave him behind.

Was it too soon? Was she sex drunk? Or was this the real thing?

She needed to walk to clear her head, that was the answer. The Verdant Sector had to be open around now, and the flowers could keep her company.

That was the plan, at least, until there was a knock at her door and it slid open to reveal Remy holding a small suitcase. The woman had a serious look on her face as she held out the bag for Zoe to take.

"Your transport is being prepared," Remy informed her. "Pack your bag and you'll be on your way back to Earth within the hour."

"What?" The bag slipped out of her fingers, and she had to stoop to pick it up. "What are you talking about? Where's Asher?" They were supposed to spend the night together. Things had changed between them. This thing was *real,* even if it was supposed to be temporary. "I'm not supposed to go home for another two weeks."

"Things have changed," Remy informed her cooly. "Pack. I'll escort you to the transport."

"There's been some kind of misunderstanding." Was Remy playing the protective family member? Did she think Zoe wasn't good enough for Asher? Maybe rich people were all the same, no matter what part of the universe you were sitting in. "I'm talking to Asher." She rushed out of the room faster than Remy could stop her.

Asher would make this right. He didn't want her to go.

His office door was unlocked when she got there, panting a bit from the speed walk. Remy was hot on her heels.

Asher sat behind his desk, a folder with a strange seal in his hands. He looked pale. And angry.

And that seal was familiar.

Zoe took a step closer and gasped when she recognized it. The seal from the game! She'd seen it in the offices when she'd signed the release forms. Did Asher have something to do with the game? Was he playing some part in this?

"I can see by your expression that you know," he said, flipping the folder shut and setting it down on the desk. Any of the light, the humor, the... love... was gone from his expression, and he stared at her like he didn't know her.

Worse. He stared at her like he hated her.

She opened her mouth to say something, but he spoke over her.

"I don't know what you were planning, but you've been found out. Go home, Miss Gershwin. Whatever you're looking for, you won't find it here." He looked past Zoe and nodded at Remy.

Remy placed a hand on her shoulder. "Come on, don't make me call in security."

"Asher—" Zoe had to say something.

But her dragon wouldn't look at her.

To hell with that. If he wasn't even going to let her explain herself or whatever this misunderstanding was, she wasn't going to beg. She turned around and marched out.

Back in her room, she stuffed the few items of clothing she'd collected into her bag. It wasn't much, and it wasn't hers, but Remy wasn't stopping her from taking it.

Zoe spotted the bag of gems that Asher had given her in payment for this façade. She'd stuffed them in the back of the drawer and forgotten about them completely. She pulled the bag out and felt the weight settle in her hand. It would serve him right if she took them. She'd earned them, hadn't she?

But her stomach roiled at the thought. This hadn't been for that. She didn't want his money.

She just wanted him.

Zoe put the bag down and saw that there was a small pad of paper and a pen on the bedside table.

He didn't deserve an explanation. She didn't need to make excuses.

But her hand was reaching for the pen of its own volition, scribbling out the words she hadn't been able to say. After a moment, she slammed the pen down and glared at the paper.

She wasn't going to hand the note to Remy. She wouldn't ask her to give it to Asher.

Zoe left it there along with the pile of rubies. If Asher saw it, he saw it.

But she wasn't going to stay where she wasn't wanted.

She grabbed her bag and followed Remy to the waiting transport. Her fairytale romance was over.

CHAPTER FOURTEEN

Asher had nothing to do. He stared at the comm screen in front of him, his calendar pulled up, and searched for any kind of task, but they were all done.

"Remy!" This was his damned sister's doing. Ever since he'd let her take charge for those two days that he did *not* think about, she'd butted her head in and made sure he was delegating.

The place was running more smoothly than ever, he had free time, and he wanted to stick his head into a meatgrinder and scream until his voice was shredded to bits.

His office door cracked open and Remy stuck her head in. "What? Don't yell."

"It's my office, I'll yell if I want." It came out petulant and made him want to curse. Everything had been fine until she showed up. He knew what he wanted, knew what he had to do.

Now there was nothing.

"What do you want?" Remy asked. "I'm busy."

"Well, I'm not. Did you have something to do with that? My calendar is clear." He jabbed his finger at the screen as if it offended him.

"We talked about that. Once a week your calendar will be clear in the afternoon so you have some time to relax. Remember?" She gave him a pointed stare.

"When did we talk about that? I need something." A puff of smoke billowed around him, and Asher took a deep, sooty, breath before he got worse. He'd been in a bear of a mood for the last week, and Remy had taken the worst of it. He couldn't decide whether or not he felt bad about that.

His career was a joke. He hated this place. Everything he'd done for the past year was for a woman he didn't like on the thin hope that she'd allow him to stay here once it was more than a sandy rock in the sky.

Money wasn't the issue. It was piling up in his account back on Vemion, both his paltry salary and the hefty income from some ancient relative's inheritance. His family would welcome him with open arms if he walked away, and Remy would jump for joy if he gave the job to her. She thrived in it.

He suffered.

And his mate was out there.

Was she back on Earth yet? He wasn't sure how long the journey was, but she had to be close to home by now. Was she happy to be rid of him? Or did she feel like he did, as if her heart had been ripped out of her chest and like she couldn't quite gulp down a sufficient breath?

The anger from the misunderstanding had faded almost as soon as she was gone, and he would have called her back if Lady Nova hadn't chosen that moment to demand a conference call with the king. She'd complimented his work and strongly suggested that he would be the right candidate for Lord-Governor when the time came.

Everything he thought he wanted was in his grasp.

All he wanted was Zoe.

"Are you okay, Ash?" Remy slid into a seat and placed her elbows on his desk, leaning down on them. "You don't look great. Have you been sleeping?"

He'd only spent one night in a bed beside his mate,

but now his own bed felt far too empty to countenance. Of course he hadn't been sleeping. He just glared at his sister.

She pursed her lips for a moment and then reached a hand into her pocket and pulled out a small notebook which she slid over to him. She reached into her other pocket and pulled out a familiar black bag, the one he'd won off of Knox and given to Zoe in payment. "Miss Gershwin left this in her room. I thought you might want it."

He snatched them from her. "When?"

Remy shrugged.

He might have demanded more, but instead he placed the bag of gems on the table and opened the notebook, looking for some clue, some hint of... something. He was the one who'd sent her away, he was the reason she was gone. He knew her planet, her name, what ship she'd traveled on. He didn't need clues to search her out.

But he wanted a piece of her.

He flipped the notebook open to a random page and saw a collection of doodles and equations that he couldn't make any sense of. But it was Zoe's handwriting, Zoe's personality in the star with a very angry face.

His mate.

He wanted to devour the text and savor it at once. He wanted to summon her back with a snap of his fingers and apologize for being an ass.

He flipped to the final page of the notebook and groaned.

"What is it?" Remy leaned forward, trying to take a look.

Asher shielded the page from view, both to keep this piece of Zoe to himself and out of shame for how stupid he'd been.

That symbol you showed me was the same one as in the game. You should have listened.

She was right. He'd known he should have given her a chance to speak from the first. But he'd been so angry—mostly at the matchmaker—and Zoe had been right there to take the brunt of it.

"Are you going to get her back?" Remy asked.

He wanted to jump out of his seat and take the next transport, to find Zoe, sweep her off her feet, and never be parted from her again.

But he should have *listened*. And he could cross half the universe and declare everything in his heart, but that wouldn't give her a reason to take him back and give him a chance.

No, he needed to earn that.

"Well?" his sister prompted.

He needed to be worthy of Zoe, needed her to understand that she was important. And he needed to be quick about it.

"I need an environmental impact report."

CHAPTER FIFTEEN

Two Weeks Later

Zoe had to quit grad school.

She'd slotted back into her life as if nothing had happened. As far as she could tell, no one had noticed that she'd gone missing for nearly a month. All her bills were on automatic payment, she didn't have a pet (thankfully!), and it was summer. As far as anyone was concerned, she'd been on vacation.

The fact that she wasn't relieved by that was a sign that things were going bad. She'd been disappointed that she hadn't been dropped from her program. Disappointed that her entire life wasn't up in flames. How messed up was that?

She hated the work she was supposed to be doing.

It was boring and tedious, and she already knew beyond a shadow of a doubt that alien life existed, she didn't need to prove it.

Zoe had been back home longer than she'd been with Asher, but the man had burrowed deep into her soul.

Mate.

She wasn't sure exactly what that meant. She'd tried to ask the curmudgeonly captain who flew her from VMC12 back to Earth, but they'd exchanged maybe fifty words in the week's long journey. Certainly nothing about mates.

But that was what Asher was to her. It wasn't a game, it wasn't fake. He was deep in her soul, the one being in the entire universe who was exactly right for her.

How many light years away was he right now?

That kind of travel was supposed to be impossible. Einstein would be rolling over in his grave. The fact that Zoe wasn't trying to understand the physics of the thing was another sign that her studies were wasted on her.

She didn't want math. She wanted her dragon lord.

Had he forgotten her?

Her phone beeped, reminding her of a meeting with her advisor in half an hour. Zoe groaned. She had no research to share, obviously, and no passion to speak of. She knew she should cancel the meeting and inform her advisor she was withdrawing from the program, but that felt so final.

What was she supposed to be if she wasn't an astrophysicist? What did people *do* outside of grad school?

Maybe she could hunt down those IDA people and see if they were hiring. She wasn't happy with the whole kidnapping thing, but she wanted to see the galaxy. Now that she'd had a taste, she wanted to know what was out there.

If she could disappear for a month, clearly no one would notice if she left for good. A depressing thought. And freeing in its own way. She wasn't stuck here. She could find something else, even if she didn't know what.

She'd walked by the building where it had all started, but the place had been stripped, not a piece of furniture or paper left to be seen.

She had to figure out *something*, because clearly the life she'd planned for herself wasn't the one she wanted. She just had to find the courage to take that first step.

Someone knocked on her door.

Zoe checked the clock, but her meeting with her advisor was still more than twenty minutes off and she'd be going to his office, not the other way around.

"Come in!" she called, though her office was barely bigger than a closet—and not the walk-in kind —and her guest would have to stand in the doorway to talk to her.

Her heartbeat kicked up for some reason, her palms tingling. What was this nervousness? It was probably someone in her cohort who needed to borrow a pen.

It was Asher.

Zoe's mouth dropped open as she took in the dragon lord standing in her doorway in jeans and a t-shirt, looking almost like a normal college student. She had to blink a few times, just to make sure she wasn't hallucinating.

This couldn't be.

"H-how?" She wanted to pull him inside and shut the door, but then they'd be standing too close together. If she touched him… well, there wasn't enough room to get up to any funny business in the office, but with Asher she might be tempted to try.

"I read your note," he said. He tried to take a step

closer, but bumped against a pile of books on the floor.

"My note. Oh. Right." It had been impulse to write it down, the simple explanation he hadn't let her give. "It's been nearly a month." Even with the travel time to get to Earth, he'd sat on that information for awhile. "Is this because of your boss? Was she upset your alleged fiancée ran away?"

His face scrunched up in confusion for a moment before he shook his head. "I quit my job. Honestly, I hated it. I was doing it for the wrong reasons and I would have been miserable if I stayed. I had to establish the sanctuary for the lizkats before I left, otherwise I would have been here sooner, but that took a bit longer than anticipated."

"What?" Her thoughts bounced around, trying to follow what he was saying. He'd quit? He'd saved the lizard-kitties? "What are you talking about?"

"I designated an area of VMC12 that won't be terraformed. We're, well, Remy now, is moving breeding pairs of lizkats into the sanctuary. The only way to save them all would be to stop all development on the planet, and that won't happen. But I could save the species. I thought you—well, I thought it was the right thing to do."

"Did you save a species for me?" The animals were

cute, sure, and her heart had hurt for the loss of them, but she hadn't considered that he might do something about it.

"I feel like I'm supposed to say this was a heartfelt action I took because I cared about the lizkats, but yes, I did it for you. Not that I'll undo it if you..."

"If I what?" They shouldn't be having this conversation where anyone could hear. Then again, her office was tucked away in a basement hallway where few dared to tread.

"I'd hoped that you would give me a second chance. There's so much more to the galaxy. You've only seen VMC12, let me show you the rest." His eyes flared with fire, a heat she could feel rumbling deep inside of her. "You're my mate, Zoe. Be with me."

Popular media would tell her she should play hard to get, to make Asher work for it a bit. But he'd saved a population of animals for her and traveled across the galaxy. As far as she was concerned, that was enough hard work.

She smiled. "Let's head back to my place."

Zoe took just enough time to send an email to her advisor to cancel their meeting. She'd figure out the rest of it later, but right now she wanted to soak up this time with Asher and find out what came next. She took the dragon's hand and led him out of the building and down the street to her apartment building.

It wasn't much, certainly not compared to what a dragon lord might have, but it was hers.

And, thankfully, it was mostly clean. She'd been stress-cleaning for two weeks as she processed everything she'd been through.

Asher looked around, taking in the second-hand couch and the prints on the wall that she'd taken from another grad student who was clearing out their apartment. The place was... eclectic, but she didn't hate it. Right now, though, the only thing in the apartment she could look at was Asher.

Their eyes met.

He grinned.

She smiled.

Then she stepped forward, wrapped her arms around his neck, and kissed him with all the pent up desire she'd been banking for the last three weeks.

He pulled her close and deepened the kiss, the fire of his tongue teasing her own.

She wanted to take her time, to explore every part of him. But it was like the floodgates had opened. Zoe tugged him towards the bedroom, unwilling to take her lips from his, but needing the space—and privacy—to strip off her clothes. She was too aware the curtain on the window wasn't drawn, and she didn't want anyone peeking inside. Asher was hers, and only hers. She needed to see him.

All alone.

And naked.

With a growl, she yanked his shirt up and over his head, exposing the gorgeous planes of his chest. He took care of his own pants, and her clothes went just as quickly. It was more hurried than sexy, but with the desperation coursing through her, she didn't care.

She couldn't stop looking at him. His eyes were burning with his inner flame, that evidence that there was nothing human about him, and that he was exactly who she needed.

He reached out and wrapped his arm around her, pulling her in tight against his chest. His cock pressed against her belly, the hard length making her shudder. She was already wet, her core aching with the need to have him.

But Asher wanted to take his time. The monster.

He backed her towards the bed and lowered her down gently, the contrast with the frantic rush to get naked sending a shiver racing down her spine.

"I've been dreaming about this, about you." He bent down and ran his tongue over one nipple, and she bit back a moan. Her breasts ached, and her hands clutched his shoulders, needing to anchor herself.

She gasped as he licked her. "Every night," she managed to say, and hoped he knew what she meant.

She was his. She'd known it on VMC12. Known it when he sent her away. Known it every moment since then. And if he tried to walk away again, it might break her.

The fear wasn't enough to keep her from touching him. No, the only thing that could do that was not having him at all.

As he suckled on one nipple, his fingers trailed down her ribs, across her hips, and along her thigh, sending sparks bursting over her skin. Everywhere he touched burned. This was going to consume her. And she wanted the flame.

He was a creature of fire, and his touch lit her up.

His fingers trailed back up her thigh, and then he cupped her, his finger brushing against her slit. She moaned, and her back arched as he ran his fingers over her, and the pleasure sent her senses whirling.

"I love the sounds you make," Asher said. He shifted his attention, trailing kisses down her stomach.

"Don't stop," she panted. She didn't even care that

the words were needy and desperate, because he was her mate, and she needed him.

Zoe reached out and threaded her fingers through his hair, tugging him closer. His laugh was low and dark, the heat of his breath sending sparks skittering across her skin.

She couldn't help herself. She needed him, and she wouldn't have been able to stop. Not when his hands were moving, his tongue licking, his fingers doing devious things to her.

His mouth found the core of her and Zoe moaned, her eyes closing as the pleasure swept her under. He licked and sucked, his tongue driving her mad, and her body was aflame.

His tongue swirled around her clit, and she clenched, her body on the edge.

She wanted to come, and she couldn't help the way her hips were bucking, pressing her body into his face, but he grabbed her and held her still, forcing her to endure the sweet torment.

It was too much.

Her heart thundered in her chest, her entire being consumed by the fire and the pleasure, and when he slid his fingers inside her, the world shattered.

Her orgasm hit her like a wildfire, her entire body spasming as the waves of pleasure washed over her.

"I need you," he panted out between kisses against her skin, dragging his body over hers, the weight of him pressing her down into the bed.

His cock pressed against her, the blunt head hot, and she arched, desperate to have him inside of her.

"I'm yours," she whispered.

"I am yours, Zoe, your mate. Always." His words were reverent, and the heat in her chest this time had nothing to do with fire, with sex. It was pure emotion, something she could only feel for this man.

He slid inside her slowly, her body adjusting, and her breath shuddered out of her. She wanted him. Needed him. "Yes." She breathed it out.

"Say it," he murmured, his mouth against her ear, and his teeth nibbling the tender skin.

"You're mine."

Asher buried himself inside her, the pleasure overwhelming, and she was lost. She clutched him close, her legs wrapped around his waist, and he thrust.

The world disappeared. All that mattered was the two of them, and the passion that consumed her. Her body shook as she came, and then he groaned, his muscles trembling as he joined her.

A grin spread wide across Zoe's face as Asher settled in next to her. He slung an arm around her, body fitting next to her just as perfectly as he fit inside her.

"So..." she said, tracing a finger over the subtle scales of his skin. "How does this mate thing work, exactly?"

He trailed kisses down her neck until her skin pebbled. "I can't wait to show you."

EPILOGUE

Two Months Later

Knox always went big. Right now, Asher appreciated his brother's extravagant taste, given the sumptuousness of the room and the massive bed he shared with his mate.

He kissed her awake, unwilling to slip out of bed without letting her know he was going. They'd woken up together every day since he'd found her on Earth, and it was a tradition he intended to keep for as long as he could.

She woke with a sleepy smile and tugged him down for a kiss. "Just a few more minutes," she murmured.

He wanted to crawl back in with her and greet the

morning in the pleasurable way they normally did, but he'd made a promise to Knox. "Sleep as long as you'd like. I'll bring you breakfast."

She smiled before closing her eyes and relaxing back into the bed.

Asher pulled on clothes and followed the scents of crisp meat to find his brother in the dining room. Flint was off on some mysterious mission, so Knox had the house all to himself.

"Your mate let you out of bed?" his brother teased.

Asher just smiled as he made up a plate for himself. "Your jealousy is showing, brother."

Knox laughed. "I'm going to find one, you know."

That had Asher pausing. Then he shook his head and continued fixing his food. No use feeding Knox's urge to be cryptic when there was bacon to be had.

When he realized Asher wouldn't bite, Knox added, "I've signed up for the IDA. I convinced Flint to do it, too. Not with that lady you went with, apparently she's booked up through the year. But I got a notice they're sending someone my way soon. She may even be my mate."

"Or another diamond to add to your hoard." Knox had just purchased a massive diamond at auction which weighed more than a kilogram and was as clear as glass. He was preparing the display case for it and was talking about holding a gala to show the thing off.

Asher and Zoe would be long gone by then, off on their tour of a nearby planetary system. His mate wanted to see the universe, and Asher would show it to her.

"We all need our hobbies," Knox responded. "Perhaps my mate would like to be draped in jewels."

"Whoever your mate is, she'll surprise you." And if she was anything like Zoe, she'd knock Knox's life completely off kilter. They'd have to come by to see it.

"You finally look happy," said Knox.

Asher smiled. "I am." He heard footsteps on the stairs and smiled even brighter as Zoe came down to join them. He rose from his chair and met her at the entryway to give her another kiss.

"Good morning," she said, smiling back at him before she pulled away.

"With you, always."

Thank you for reading Asher!

The series continues with *Knox*.

Read now!

KEEP IN TOUCH!

Want a little bit more of Zoe & Asher? Get a free bonus
scene where Asher gets a taste of life on Earth!
Sign up now

Ready to give audio a try? Get a free audiobook here!

WHAT TO READ NEXT: KNOX

A wannabe reformed thief and a dragon lord looking for love...

After witnessing the skills of the Intergalactic Dating Agency at finding mates, Knox enlists their services to find a woman of his own. He's collected a hoard of precious stones from across the galaxy, a mate will be his crown jewel. But is he looking for love, or another treasure for his collection?

Fresh off a prison colony, Aria wants to go straight. But when her past catches up to her, her only choice to escape a gnarly fate is to infiltrate Knox's home and steal a gigantic diamond right from under his nose. She's got the perfect cover: the Intergalactic Dating Agency.

But as she gets closer to the fiery dragon lord, the

last thing she wants to do is betray him as he rouses feelings in her she never knew she could feel. When Knox finds out the truth, will he help her or will the betrayal be too much to overcome?

How can she keep her dragon mate and escape her past?

JOIN THE CELESTIAL HEARTS CLUB

Hey there, **wonderful reader! Are you ready to take our relationship to the next level?**

By becoming a member of the Celestial Hearts Club, you'll get access to:

- early access to chapters from books before they're published
- exclusive short stories - at least one a month!
- sneak peeks that will make your heart skip a beat

Plus, you'll be directly contributing to the creation of more epic love stories and heart pounding space adventures.

Are you ready to hop on board and support the creation of more out-of-this-world romance?

Check it out!

https://katerudolph.net/celestialheartsclub

INTERGALACTIC DATING AGENCY

LOOKING for love that's out of this world? These strong, smart, sexy aliens are seeking mates from the Milky Way. Just hop onboard with your local Intergalactic Dating Agency. Join our group of authors as we explore the friendly skies and beyond with trilogies of cosmic craving, astral adventure, and otherworldly lovers. Warning: abductions may or may not be included!

ALSO BY KATE RUDOLPH

Dragon Brides
Dragon Princes. Fierce Women. Love.
Fated mates, fierce women, and dragon princes are ready to find their mates.

Crux

Ranger

Saber

Cipher

Storm

Drake

Asher

Knox

Flint

———

Guarded by the Shifter

Werewolf. Bodyguard. Mate.

The origins of these shifters are shrouded in mystery, but they're determined to protect their mates from any harm that comes their way.

Also available in audio!

Hunting Season

On the Prowl

Stalking Magic

Hungry for the Wolf

Wolf Cursed (novella)

Wolf's Temptation

———

Stealing the Alpha

The thief takes what she wants, but the alpha keeps what's his...

Join shifter thief Mel as she clashes with lion alpha Luke in an explosive trilogy of two opposites who can't keep away from one another.

Also available in audio!

The Alpha Heist

Entangled with the Thief
In the Alpha's Bed

Alien Mates: Planet Exile

Guerran is no place for pretty human women. But these alien heroes will protect their mates!
Also available in audio!

Exile's Hunter
Exile's Adored

Zulir Warrior Mates

Kidnapped humans. Alien Warriors. Electric wings.
The Zulir Warrior Mates series brings you human heroines and heroes abducted from Earth who find love – and wings! – with the alien warriors who rescue them.
Also available in audio!

Synnr's Saint
Synnr's Hope
Synnr's Spark
Synnr's Kiss
Synnr's Ride

Mated to the Alien

Fated Mate Alien Romance
Detyens are doomed to die young if they don't find their fated mates.
Follow along as these mated pairs fight off aliens, corrupt dictators, prejudiced humans, pirates, and more! The books can be read or listened to in any order, though some characters show up in multiple stories.
Select books available in audio.
Pick a book and jump into the action today!
Ruwen

Tyral

Stoan

Cyborg

Krayter

Kayleb

Shayn

Braxtyn

Doryan

Dekon

Detyen Warriors

Detya was destroyed a hundred years ago. These doomed warriors are out to find justice… and their mates.

The Detyen Warriors series brings you kick butt heroines, alpha alien heroes, fated mates, and relationships strong enough to span the galaxy!

The entire series is also available in audio!

Soulless

Ruthless

Heartless

Faultless

Endless

Alien Holiday Romance

Christmas... in space????
These alien holiday romances look beyond Earth's winter holidays and ring in the season across the galaxy!
Select titles available in audio.
Snowed in with the Alien Beast
The Alien's Winter Gift
The Alien Reindeer's Wild Ride
Trapped with her Alien Mate

———

Alien Outlaws

Outlaws, schemes, and love... it's all there in the Alien Outlaws series...

Andie Munster is sick of life on Ixilta, the planet she got dumped on after being abducted from Earth six years ago. And when the mysterious and dangerous Xandr shows up looking for a way off the planet, she's half-prisoner, half-co-conspirator in a wild rush to escape.

Rogue Alien's Escape
Rogue Alien's Woman
Rogue Alien's Secret
Rogue Alien's Legacy

Find more by Kate Rudolph at www.katerudolph.net

ABOUT KATE RUDOLPH

KATE RUDOLPH IS a paranormal and sci-fi romance writer who lives in Indiana. She loves writing about kick butt heroines and the steamy heroes who love them. She's been devouring romance novels since she was too young to be reading them and had to hide her books so no one would take them away. She couldn't imagine a better job in this world than writing romances and sharing them with her fellow readers.

If you enjoyed this story, please consider leaving a review.